The Hip-Hop Series

Word Works by, for and in the Language of the New Urban Generation

Www.PenknifePress.Com

One
Dead
Doctor

One Dead Doctor
A David Price Mystery
by
Tony Lindsay

Penknife Press   Chicago, Illinois

This is a work of fiction. The characters, dialogue and events described herein are the products of the author's imagination, and do not portray actual persons or events.

ISBN 978-1-59997-012-7

Library of Congress Control Number: 2012930236

Manufactured in the United States of America

Acknowledgments

A heartfelt thank you to my close readers: Roy Mock and Florine Weston.

For my mother,
Sadie B. Davis

Love you, mama.

Chapter One

I am too tired to deal with what is before me. My brother is sitting at the kitchen table whining, no, crying over a woman. A woman he went to a drug treatment program with because both him and her had smoked up their damn lives. But what I do not understand . . . is how are two people with same damn problem going to help each other. He smokes crack-cocaine and she smokes crack-cocaine; them helping each other is insane, but what do I know.

The young woman, Nikki, has worried my brother stupid for the past three weeks. Since the day they were released from treatment, he has been overly concerned about her making meetings, her going to groups, and her doing whatever else crack-heads do to stop using that shit. I think he should be concentrating on himself because my brother is getting old. He is way too old to be running up and down the streets being a crack-head and chasing behind a girl less than half his age. I would hand him a dishtowel to wipe his tears, but I don't want his snot on my clean towels.

My brother's newly sober state of mind has him off kilter. He's not himself. He's become too emotional and way too sensitive. The man is wearing his heart on his sleeve, big time. And it's not just the young woman. He is sensitive about everything. Any silly little joke hurts his feeling.

Three days ago he dropped something fierce in the toilet. I'm talking paint peeling funky. When I walked into the bathroom after him, the scent from his excretion was so thick it took my breath away. I had to make an immediate u-turn.

I told him, "Man . . . weapons of mass destruction ain't got a thing

1

on you partner. You could clear an urban area with one of them dumps."

Before going to drug treatment, my brother would have vamped right back on me. But this post treatment brother of mine went into a spiel about how he has polluted his system with narcotics over the years, and how he hopes his bodily odors aren't too offensive. Then, his curly head dropped, and his shoulders slumped like he was going through a thing . . . over a joke.

The truth of the matter was that the funk wasn't related to narcotic impurities; the night before we ate White Castles. He had a sack of ten. I had a sack of ten, and his little bow legged Nikki had half a sack. That's all it was. The remains of grilled onions and beef patties made the horrific odor, but he took it deeper. Everything that's said to him has to have an underlying meaning. He no longer accepts statements at face value.

I love my brother, even if he is sitting across from me sucking snot up his nose like a little kid, and I am overjoyed about what he is trying to do with his life. No way is the crack smoking Robert wanted back in whole; I just want parts of him back. Like the part that could take a joke, and the part that didn't get weepy over women. My brother has lived off of and with women since he was seventeen years old. He is not a man who sobs about a female. Well . . . at least he wasn't.

Looking from my teary-eyed brother to my gold Rolex, I see it is three forty five in the a.m., and I just finished a thirteen-hour drive from D.C. The last thing I am in the mood for is a damn near fifty-year-old man sniveling like an eight year old boy who lost his puppy. A thirteen-hour drive is a long chore even in a BMW 745i.

Through his sniffles, I hear him saying, "We was suppose to start over together man. Me and her and this new drug free life. We talked about how hard it was going to be, but we was gonna be there for each other. Keep each other clean."

He blows his nose into a napkin from the holder on the table. My Dobermans are asleep at his feet. I hear them readjusting their sleeping positions after the honker from his nose. I stand from the table and go to the sink.

I pour out what is left of the coffee from my thermos and rinse it out. The strong day old coffee smells through the kitchen. My back is to my brother while standing at the sink. I like this double-sided chrome sink with the stainless steel trim because nothing sticks to it; everything rinses down the drain. I cut the water off and think about my big bed.

If I would have gone straight upstairs, and not came back to the kitchen, I might have missed hearing this drama and been asleep. My brother is sitting at our grandmother's kitchen table which is one of the few items left in the house that was hers. As sweet as she was, she was not one to coddle and neither am I.

Not wanting too, but to show some brotherly concern I ask, "When was the last time you saw her?"

I leave the top off my thermos and place it upside in the dish rack.

"Day before yesterday, she was here when you and Ricky left for D.C., remember?"

Yeah she was here. They were sitting in the living area on my brushed lambskin couch eating rib tips. Juicy, hickory smoked, and tender looking rip tips. I didn't ask them to move to the kitchen because my thinking was and is that for addicts trying to live without using drugs life is hard. And they don't need people stressing them out

3

over little things. My complaining about them eating ribs on my couch was a little thing, and I did not and do not want to be a stressor to either of them. So I let them sit on my lambskin couch and watch my big screen television while eating grease laden but damn good smelling barbecued pork, and neither one of them offered me a rib tip or a french-fry, and I wanted some, but since they didn't offer, I didn't ask.

"She left here that night for a woman's only Narcotics Anonymous meeting at the church on Sixty-Fifth Street. I went to the meeting at the health center. She was supposed to meet me there for coffee, but she didn't show up. And I ain't seen her since. Nobody has seen her. She missed two days of outpatient groups, and the social worker says if she don't hear from her tomorrow she's out of the program. And that's her money and her housing, D. If she gets kicked out of there . . . it's back to the streets for her, and I can't let that happen. I can't. We promised each other."

My brother trying to straighten out his life has our whole family happy. He has never tried before and was adamant about living his drug using life. He felt his drug usage was no different than people smoking cigarettes or drinking alcohol. He argued that mood-altering substances were all the same, and that there was no difference between nicotine and cocaine. However, after fifteen years of smoking crack-cocaine his opinion has finally changed. He now believes crack-cocaine does more damage than cigarettes or alcohol to a person's mind, body, and spirit.

My grandmother left this house to my brothers and me. Neither of them wanted to live in it, so I bought it from them. I gave each thirty thousand dollars for their part. Robert went through the money in less than six months. That's when he started talking about maybe going to get help. It took another year and a half before he actually went to rehab.

I turn from the sink and walk back to the table. My brother is not crying anymore. I strip my double holster off and hang the .9mms across the back of the chair, and sit at the table with him.

"So what are you thinking?"

He is dressed in one of the long sleeved pullover sweaters I gave him, the black one.

"I need you to go to a couple of dope spots with me. I can't go by myself. If I walk in one of them places alone I'll start using. I know it, but if you go with me . . . I can lean on you and go in and get out. If I hesitate, I know you will snatch me up out of there, D. I wouldn't pull you into this, man, if my worry wasn't strong. It's not just that she might be getting high, but two girls have turned up dead these past weeks. Chicks that was in the treatment program with us."

I had heard about one girl before we left for D.C. It was rumored that she was found naked behind a liquor store with a black ribbon around her neck.

"Are they saying the second girl had a ribbon around her neck?" My hope is he says no.

"Yep, that's what the word is, a black one just like the one they found on Tasha. And the second girl, Lynette, she wasn't nothing but twenty two. And Tasha was around the same age."

Now I understand his concern. The girls being in treatment with him and Nikki, and the dead girls being around the same age as Nikki puts the deaths and maybe even the killer close. I know the answer, but I ask, "When do you want to start looking for her?"

He stands, and I see that he has ironed a sharp crease in the khaki work pants Mama sent him.

"I got to find her tonight man and get her to our out-patient groups tomorrow."

"You mean today. It's already tomorrow."

His eyes go past me to the window and out into the blackness of the early morning. He looks more like my father than either my brother Charles or me. Robert has the same dark muscular face and pug nose as my father.

"Yeah today, right now really."

He runs his hand through the black curly hair my mother gave him, "It won't take us long man. She's close. I can feel her."

Standing puts me eye to eye with him. We are all the same height: my father, Robert, Charles, and me. We all stand six feet two inches tall. Robert would probably be taller if his knees weren't knocked, and the drug using life style has thinned him. I doubt that he weighs a hundred eighty pounds.

To him I say, "You risking a lot for this young woman."

I strap my pistols back on.

"It was a promise man and . . . I love her . . . fo' real."

I do not comment on his confessed love. My mouth wants to. My brain wants to, but I do not. It's hard for a man to warn another man against a woman. Women affect a man's logic through physical comfort and emotional support. And with him wearing his heart on his sleeve, he won't hear my warning. Saying nothing is best, at least for now, especially with his girl being in possible danger.

Two murdered girls in the same neighborhood is fucked up. No question about it, but two under the same circumstances, both being addicts, is damn dangerous. The killer has no fear, a deadly appetite, and a preferred choice of victim. Like her or not, we need to find his bowlegged woman, and I pray that we find her alive. My brother wouldn't handle her death well. He is committed to Nikki, and their relationship obviously started before treatment.

I knew nothing of her prior to meeting her on family day at the rehab center. There he introduced her as his 'little boo'. She is the only woman he has introduced to me with any form of endearment his entire adult life.

He has been living with me for three weeks, and for the most part, I can hardly tell when he is in the house. He's gone to groups and twelve step meetings all day. And when he is home, his head is buried in those Narcotics' Anonymous books or the Bible. He's always reading and writing. He says part of his changing is learning who he is. The same addict will use again he told me. So he has to change, and all the reading and writing is helping him change.

I see that he is trying, and I think that his missing woman may be in real danger. I told his social worker and my parents that I would do all that was within my power to help him. So, tired or not, I got to move. My brother needs me.

Strapping up my pistol harness I say, "Let's roll man. Yin, Yang, come."

My Dobermans spring to life from under my grandmama's kitchen the table.

Chapter Two

My brother doesn't want to drive around in the car and look for his girl, no, that would be too easy. He's saying, "We might drive by her in a car, D. She's around here somewhere. I know it. Walking through the 'hood is the best way."

So I have to go back into the house and get my Sox jacket to cover my pistols. I close the front door of my house and follow him down the porch steps. Yin and Yang are already at the bottom of the stairs with their stubby tails just a jumping. At least they're happy about the early a.m. walk through the 'hood. And if my brother had a stubby tail, his would be wagging too.

"Thanks for this man," he says, "let's go to the Reeds' first. Nikki ain't the type of woman to wander outside of where she is comfortable. She didn't leave the 'hood."

He's walking and talking at the same time. We cross the street and are walking north down the block to the Reeds'.

Our block is filled with two story frame houses, and each has steps leading up to a porch. Most of the houses have small patch lawns surrounded by chain link fences. It's going to be a chilly fall day. A jacket is needed out here in the early morning with no sun.

The early morning mist has the black top of the street shining, and it sends a chill across the top of my shaved head. The peachy street lights illuminate the street and sidewalks, but the gangways between the houses are dark. Our walk has set off a couple of motion sensor porch lights. Two cats dart across Yin and Yang's path. Neither flinches in the felines' directions. They are happy to be out, but they know the walk has a purpose. My boys are well trained.

The Reeds' gangway is dimly lit by light from the basement windows. There is only enough light to stop one from tripping over the cracked sidewalk.

"We got to go to the basement door," my bother says as if I don't know.

He couldn't have forgotten the numerous times I drug him from this house. That was back when I thought I could make a person stop being a crack-head. Man, he and I had some fights.

"They ain't gonna let the dogs in, D."

"They ain't gonna have a choice. Ain't nobody gonna be at the door but Melvin, Nathan, or Tim and we been beating them down their whole lives."

The statement makes my bother open up a grin that can be seen in the dim light of the gangway. Before he got cracked out, neither of the Reeds boys could out box him. The fact is, he used to take their lunch money. I walk down the stairs with my dogs at my side and rap on the door.

"Yeah," is said in reply to my hard knock.

I answer, "It's Price," knowing they will think it's my brother.

The door opens, and I push my way in with one pistol drawn.

"Aw shit, it's the crazy one!" is my greeting.

I tell my dogs, "Secure," and they hold cross-eyed Nathan Reeds against the gray brick wall behind the door. Not hesitating, I enter the common area of the basement. I was expecting a crowded smoke filled area, but only four men are sitting at a table with tiny plastic bags of crack in front of them. I guess Sunday night slash Monday morning is not a popular time for crack smoking.

Two of the four were in the middle of taking hits from their crack pipes. The other two, with eyes fixed on my pistol, are trying to gather their drugs.

"Stop moving," is my order.

Nobody at the table poses any threat.

Behind the bar I see bald headed Melvin Reeds with a shotgun in front of him. The weapon is on the top of the bar.

The bar looks real familiar to me for some reason. It's not the whole bar that's familiar, just the top. It's covered with the same lime green and yellow floor tiles that I have on my back porch. In the spring my brother tiled my porch, and I knew there should have been some leftover boxes.

I cock the hammer on my .9mm in response to the wanting I see in Melvin's eyes. He wants the rifle, bad. I shake my head no and say, "You know I don't like ya ass. Reach for that weapon and we won't have to worry about liking each other no mo'."

He steps back from the rifle.

Nikki is on the couch passed out. My brother runs to her and picks her up.

"All you had to do was ask for the bitch. Damn Price, we wasn't holding the ho' hostage or nothing," Melvin says to Robert.

Nikki wakes up and clings to my brother. He has her in his arms and moves for the door. I am behind him. When we exit I walk out without calling my dogs, leaving Nathan pinned to the wall.

"Man ya dogs! Shit, call ya damn dogs," Nathan yells at our backs.

Instead of calling my dogs I tell them to, "Speak to him", causing them to growl, snarl, and bark as if they are going to attack. Yin, the oldest is a red Doberman, and he likes to attack.

"Man ya dogs, get ya damn dogs!" he begs.

11

"Yin, Yang, come."

Yang obeys, but Yin requires a second call, "Yin come!"

And now they are both with us on the brisk walk home.

*

Getting his young lover didn't take fifteen minutes total. I accept my brother's and his girlfriend's timid thanks and make it up to my California king sized bed. In my room, I strip down to my white boxer briefs and drop to the bed.

I say a prayer of thanks with my head on the pillow. I thank Him for the girl being alive and for us getting home safe. And while I'm talking to God, I bring up my best friend Ricky and ask the Lord to help him.

We drove to D.C., so Ricky could see an herbalist who specializes in herbs for the heart. My best friend of thirty plus years is sick. He thinks the heart medicine his regular doctor gave him is responsible for his jones not getting hard. He said he never had the problem until he started taking the medicine.

Ricky went to the internet looking for alternatives to the prescribed medicine and found the herbalist in D.C., so we drove down there for him to get examined by the herb doctor. The doctor gave him some dried roots, some pills, and some teas, and told him to lose two hundred pounds. She told him if he didn't lose the weight he wouldn't live another three years. Ricky believed her.

He tipped the herb doctors scale to four hundred and six pounds. She told him the roots would stimulate his blood flow and help with the erectile dysfunction along with the pills. Then she gave him bags of a tea to help with his cholesterol, but the problem, she said, was his weight. She told him that impotence would be the least of his problems if he didn't start losing weight. She told him his heart was going to stop in his sleep. The little Asian doctor spoke so matter-of-factly that I got kind of angry with her.

On the drive home, Ricky's huge basketball head was bent over the diet material she gave him for most of the ride home. The herbalist not only told him to diet, in addition, she said he had to walk for at least thirty minutes a day and sweat from exercise three times a week. While talking to God, I ask Him to give Ricky strength and will power because I know my friend. Away from the herb doctor and her concise words, the statements will lose some of their sting.

I also ask the Creator to give me the necessary strength to stay diligent on encouraging my friend to diet and exercise and to help my brother stay drug free. It won't be easy, but I'm not losing my best buddy to pig ear sandwiches or my brother to crack-cocaine.

*

I wake from a dream about girls being chased by black snakes because of Robert's raised voice. He's not yelling, but he's on the brink of it.

"Where did you get the money if you wasn't out there dating. Two days is a long time to smoke with no loot."

"I had money."

"I guessed that, but where did you get it?"

"You know what I did."

"No I don't. If I knew I wouldn't be asking you."

"I got some scripts from Dr. Aims. I got 'em filled and sold the pills and the bottles methadone."

"He just gave you the scripts?"

"Well you know how he is, I had to do a little somethin' something,' but I wasn't on the streets."

I hear nothing for several moments. I stop myself from getting out of my bed and going to the bedroom door to eavesdrop better because this is my brother's business.

Then I hear a heavy sigh and, "If there is going to be a 'we' with us, a 'you and me together', you got to stop dating all together. No turning tricks."

"You didn't mind it when we was getting high."

"But we ain't getting high no more Nicki. We starting a new life. We squaring up."

"You still want a 'we' with me after yesterday and all?"

"Your slip is my fall. We in this together. I wouldn't have even went to treatment if it wasn't for you. You came to me saying enough was enough. You said it's a better life out there for us. Those were your words, Nikki. Your thoughts, you got the fire started. The least I can do is blow the flame. We in this together."

Again silence.

"It's harder than I thought Bobby. Smoking crack is part of me. Changing doesn't feel right. I feel like I am going against who I am."

"I feel that way too, but that's because we are going against what we been. We changing from people who smoke crack to people that don't. Using dope was what we did, it's what our brain and body is use to. Yeah it's hard right now. It's hard for me too, but we gonna make it. We got our Higher Power; Jesus is working with us, we gonna make it."

"Why are you so sure?"

"Cause it's time, just like you said. Now come on. We got to get to walking to be there by eight."

I hear the door close behind them. My brother's social worker said I should call her with any concerns. Nikki and his relationship is a concern. She's pulling him down. Looking over at the red digits of the clock it reads seven fifteen. I can get another two hours sleep.

*

I can think of no one who would have a reason to be ringing my doorbell at seven forty-five in the morning. The reason must be urgent because they are consistent in the pushing of the chimes. I slide back into my black jeans and stumble more than walk down the stairs.

The blue and white flashing lights are entering my home through the curtains and drapes hanging in front of my recently added bay window. Yin and Yang are at the door waiting for me to open it. Peeping through the peephole, I see the wood pulp colored face of Detective Lee. The lock wearing police officer who is dating my ex-wife, Regina. I open the big door but not the security door. His unmarked black Ford and about six blue and white squads are on the block.

"We found a body in the alley behind your house," he says over his shoulder while going down the stairs with red locks bobbing up and down, "Come on back."

The words take the tone of an order more than a request. I close the door on him and the flipping squad car lights.

Chapter Three

A clear, nippy, autumn morning meets the dogs and me at the back door. The frantic pace of the police officers and photographers lessens the chill in the air. The uniformed officers are sectioning off the area of the alley behind my house and my neighbors Fred and Bonnie.

Back in the spring, I had the dying Maple tree removed from my back yard. With the Maple tree gone, I have an unobstructed view from my back steps to the alley. Fred and Bonnie are in their yard at the back gate. Fred waves me over. I zip up my sweater, and the dogs and I go down the stairs and head in their direction.

When we get to the back gate, I see that the police are holding media crews at bay at both ends of the alley, and the space is packed with vans and people with cameras and microphones. It must be a slow news day. This amount of coverage for a death in the 'hood is unusual.

"I came out to feed the pigeons and empty the garbage this morning. I was throwing around old corn bread and crumbled end pieces when I saw her. She was laying right there in the middle of the alley."

My eyes follow the direction in which Fred's ashy finger is pointing. I see the nude back and butt of a small and I am guessing young sister. A sudden gust of wind is blowing dried red and brown leaves all over the ground and her.

"She looked young, D, too young to be dead in an alley. I ran back into the house and called the police. They were here before I could get back out there to her. I would have covered her up with a sheet or something, but once the police got here they wouldn't let me near her."

Hearing a sniffle causes me to look down into the coco brown

17

baby-doll face of Bonnie. On her face, I see the sadness this situation has caused her.

"I'm going in the house," she says gathering her trench coat around her neck, "got to get ready for work."

On her feet are a pair of men's leather slippers, and in her hair are small metal hair clips.

"The police said they wanted to talk to us," Fred says with his gaze in the alley.

"I didn't see anything. You found her not me. I'm gone." She turns from us and the alley and beelines through the yard and up the stairs into their yellow with white trim frame house.

I guess the ambulance attendant or some doctor has to pronounce the girl dead before the morgue people can come and get her. Her death is a shame, a mark on our community, and the police that protect it.

Fred blows out a long sigh and says, "Too young. She is too young to be dead on the concrete. I knew she was gone the minute I saw her. A corpse has no presence . . . I learned that in Desert Storm."

Fred is the second man I have seen teary eyed today, and I don't think either one has a reason to cry. As far as the dead girl in the alley, it is not sadness a man should feel, but anger. The community on a whole should be fuming, but especially the men. We men should be pissed the fuck off at the police and ourselves.

Our women, our children are not protected as they should be. They should be as safe on our neighborhood streets as women and children are on Downtown streets or on Lincoln Park streets or on the streets of the North Shore, but they're not. They die on our streets, and that is not something to be sad about, that is something to be pissed the

18

fuck off about.

Fred leans against the fence and says, "And from what I heard the police saying, she is the third girl they found this month," his hands are clenched on the top rail of the chain link fence. "Some maniac is out here killing girls and the police ain't telling nobody."

The paramedics around the body have shifted position and seeing the corpse in whole allows me to see what I hoped not to see; there is a black ribbon tied around her neck.

"Damn."

Turning away from the young woman's nude body, I notice my ex-wife, Regina, at the front of the media crowd. Detective Lee and his partner Dixon are talking to her. She acknowledges seeing me with a nod of her head while taking notes from the detectives.

I'm surprised she didn't just come through my house and yard to get inside the police blockade. That level of intrusiveness has become her style. She will push past a one-legged blind man to get in a question for one of her stories. Why she is standing at the blockade with the rest is a mystery to me.

An independent woman she is, but I can't help but wish she wasn't in this alley. It could turn dangerous back here. And ex-wife or not, she is the mother of my son and I want her safe. As a reporter, I am sure she is in more dangerous situations than this, but I'm not there to witness them.

She and one other reporter are now being allowed through with their cameramen. Oh, I get it. She is playing by the rules and getting privileges. That's why she waited with the others, and I'm sure dating Detective Lee is an advantage in situations like this.

"Ain't that ya ex-wife, Regina Price, from the Tribune?" Fred asks nodding his short afro in Regina's direction.

"Yep, that's her."

"It's good she's out here. If anybody will get the story to the people, she will. Folks need to know that these killings are happening. She will get to the truth, and let us know the real deal. You can bet that. She gets the job done."

Such has become her reputation in the community. People trust her reporting and rely on her column for the truth. I am proud of her for that. Her taste in men, however, yields no pride from me. We just went through a debacle of a case. One I nicknamed One Dead Lawyer that was due to her poor taste in men. Her dating the red Bob Marley, Detective Lee, isn't much better in my opinion.

Lee and his cheap-suit wearing partner Dixon have tried to pin murder charges on me before because of their lazy ass work ethic. I can't stand the sight of either one of them. Regina dating Lee has forced a smile-in-your-face,-but-will-stab-your-ass-in-the-neck relationship between him and me.

When I go to her house to get my son, I usually see Lee lurking in the background. And since a brother was raised right, I speak to his shifty ass and hold very brief one-two sentence conversations, but I part his ex-wife fucking, wanna-be-me, company as soon as possible. Standing here in the morning sun, and watching him escorting Regina through the crime scene is putting rocks in my jaws. Well, the truth of the matter is once I am angry about one thing any other irritating event merely adds to the flame.

The possibility of a child being murdered behind my house ignited the fire, add to that Lee walking around with his hand on the small of Regina's back, damn near on her ass, has a brother spitting out lava rocks. What I need to do, is stop looking at Regina and Lee and look somewhere else.

My glance goes up, to the pigeons that have landed on edges of garage rooftops. Above them, I notice the baby blue sky and the strands of cotton like clouds stretched across it. Despite the evil activity of man in the alley, the Creator has given us a beautiful morning, and seeing it does bring a little calm to my bothered mind.

The pigeons are looking down on the business of death from the garage roofs, and I am surprised they are not down here amongst the media crowd and police pecking up the bread Fred threw to them earlier because Chicago pigeons ain't scared of much. Perhaps the lack of presence in the body, death, has kept them on the roofs.

The coroner guys have arrived and are making their way to the body with a stretcher and a black tag bag. The paramedics move aside, and the morgue guys roll her over.

"Got-damnit!" I know her.

It's Babygirl, Ricky's niece Claire, his oldest sister's only child.

I am about to jump the fence, but Dixon has made it over to me. "You know her?" He asks in response to my outburst.

This man's breath is always rancid onion foul. I turn my nose from his direction and answer, "Yes. I know the young woman and the family. Her name is Claire Anderson."

He flips open his little blue spiral note pad.

"You got an address?"

They have placed Claire on the stretcher atop the black vinyl tag bag. One of the attendants is adjusting her small feet in the bag. He gets them in and with a firm grip on the zipper, "zzzzrrrip", the tag bag is closed. Her people will have to go to the county morgue to see her again.

"Her parents are Reynard and Brenda Anderson. They reside at 6811 South Peoria Street. He's an insurance broker, and she's a seamstress. They are real good people."

Still scribbling he asks, "How do you know them?"

"Brenda Anderson is Ricky Brown's sister."

"Your boy Ricky?" He stops writing and looks up me.

"Yep."

"Man, you two stay in the trenches."

He flips his little book closed, "I might as well say it now; leave this investigation to us Price. We don't want and won't need your help on this. Understand?"

Three dead girls in a week, they need somebody's damn help. I turn away from him and the stink cloud his breath has created.

"Oh God no!"

It's Regina's scream. She had the attendant open the tag bag before he put Clair into the coroner's wagon.

"David, it's Clair!"

I jump the fence and run to my ex-wife despite Lee holding her. When I get to her, she breaks his embrace and falls into my arms. In my ear she whispers, "Take me in your house, David, please."

My dogs followed me over the fence and they have cleared the area around Regina and I. Both have their attention on Detective Lee. I love my dogs.

*

As soon as I close the back door, Regina stands erect no longer leaning on me or crying. Her eyes are not red or wet. She hasn't shed a tear.

"Those bastards know we have a serial killer in the city. They are saying three because it's only been three in Englewood, but it was two more on the Westside in the Austin area last year. The same black ribbon around the girls necks, but since there were no more after the two they hushed it up.

"And they were trying to get me to not report the deaths as related and to keep the black ribbon out of the story. Screw that! The ribbon *is* the story."

She goes straight into the living area, drops down on my lambskin sofa, and pulls her laptop from her green nylon shoulder bag. She unplugs the phone line from my phone and plugs it into her laptop without taking off her trench coat.

"I got to get this in now, D. I hope you don't mind?"

She doesn't stop to see if I mind or not.

"Johnny was trying to edit my story. Can you imagine that? He was suggesting what I should include and omit. He and his troll looking partner can kiss my ass. Bastards, both of them, it was the mother of one of the dead girls from the Westside who called last week and told me about the police not investigating her daughter's death. I was looking into that case and found out about the other one on the Westside and then last week's two came across my desk, but the police knew all along.

"We got a maniac out there killing young women, and Detective Johnny Lee tells me not to panic. It's time to panic, and it's time to warn the people. Good, I'm in."

Two thousand and three technology, it's amazing to me what one can do with a laptop and a phone line. She's typing frantically on her keyboard.

23

"This morning I told the city editor that I had tomorrow's front page story. He's waiting to see if I do. Johnny didn't want me to see the ribbon around the victim's neck. I heard you tell Dixon it was Claire . . . ." she pauses.

I was beginning to wonder was it was all a roust and did she have any feelings for the girl.

"Darling Claire, last I heard she made captain of her cheerleading squad. That was what five, six years ago? She was the sweetest girl and smart if I remember correctly. I don't recall much about her parents. She was always with Ricky and his twin girls when I saw her. She didn't deserve this type of death. No woman, no child does. However, what is really raising my dander is that they knew! The police are certain that a killer is prowling our streets.

"The ribbon around her neck matched those in the photos of the Westside victims. There is a cover up in play. They are trying to hide their sloppy police work, and I'm not having it; not at the risk of public safety. The people will be warned of this situation."

With her shiny black hair hanging down blocking her face, she hasn't looked up at me once during her tirade. Her head is hanging over her laptop. She is on the trail, and I do understand that. I leave her to do her thing and go upstairs to get my cell phone since she is on my house line.

*

Sitting on the bed, I can't help but think about the five dead girls. Well, five that have been reported. Only the Lord, the killer, and his victims really know how many have died at his hands. I wonder what the actual cause of death was. I'll have to ask Regina because I didn't see any blood or a wound. No one has stated with any certainty that the girls were sexually violated. Found naked doesn't always mean raped, and what's with the black ribbons? Five dead girls, five devastated families, one of which I have to notify.

This is not a call I want to make. Being the bearer of bad news sucks, I flip open my phone and punch in his numbers.

"Hey, Ricky."

"What's up, D?"

There is no other way to do it but to say it.

"The police found Claire, dead, behind my house. I'm sorry, man."

"What Claire? Babygirl? My Claire? Dead?"

"Yes, Babygirl."

"Dead? How? What are you talkin' about man?"

"She was found behind my house in the alley."

"Damn . . . you sure it's Claire, our Babygirl? Da police sure?"

"Yeah . . . I identified her."

"You indentified her?"

"She was found behind my house, Ricky."

"Nigga, come get me. I want to see her with my own damn eyes. Fuck what you takin' 'bout."

"They've taken her to the morgue."

"Damn . . . dat's gonna tear Brenda up. Come get me, man, and carry me over my sister's house. She's gonna want to talk to you."

I need to get to my office, but I say, "See ya in a minute, bro," flipping the phone closed.

My next call should be to the office. Nope, it's better to do a drive by at least. Standing from the bed I target the bathroom to complete my daily three Ss: a shit, a shower, and a shave.

*

25

In the shower a knocking is heard, but I can't tell if it's the bedroom door, the bathroom door, or a water pipe. I pull the curtain to step out just as the door is opening. Regina sees me butt naked and wet. Her grayish green eyes are on my jones and she ain't looking away. He's starting to swell from her attention.

She turns away and says, "I was just letting you know I'm leaving," and closes the door.

I step back into the running water, pulling the curtain closed and say, "Okay."

No big deal to her, no big deal to me, but one would think it would only be polite to look a man in his face after you have looked at his dick. Give a brother a smile, a nod, a wink, a pseudo innocent 'oops' with a giggle, at least some type of acknowledgement that you just saw his jones. She peeped and ran. What kind of mess is that? Exs, damn.

After the shower, I notice the pills Ricky gave me on the sink. I asked him for a couple since he got so many from the herb doctor. I figured they should probably give me an energy boost. I'm still a little tired from not getting my proper rest last night, so I take two from the baggy and swallow them. A brother needs some type of boost.

Chapter Four

We didn't beat the police to Ricky's sister's house even with me not going into the office. I pull up alongside the dusty black detective car and park across the street from it and the family's brick bungalow home. The late morning sky is still clear, and the sun is shining through the sparse toast colored leaves of the trees.

"At least they sent detectives and not patrolmen," Ricky says looking at the unmarked black Ford. "Hope it ain't your buddies."

He's talking about Dixon and Lee, and I share his sentiment.

Having parked we exit my 745i. I get out a lot easier than my heavy friend of thirty plus years. It's about forty degrees out here perfect leather jacket weather. Ricky doesn't have on a jacket just a green short sleeve Coogi sweater, but nevertheless he is sweating. His forehead is wet with perspiration. He exhales powerfully as he frees himself from the front seat.

We bought matching seven series BMWs at the same time a couple of months ago, but Ricky traded his for a Cadillac Escalade. My guess is the big SUV gives him easier access. I wait for him to come around the car and then follow him across the street and up the porch steps.

The screen is still in the top half of the thin white aluminum door. The big wooden door is open. Ricky sister is heard questioning the police.

"Why are you asking me those type of questions? My daughter wasn't a whore or a junkie. She had a little problem, but she was working on it. She was in outpatient treatment and going to meetings. So you can stuff them type of questions where the sun don't shine.

"Matter of fact, why are you questioning me at all? You telling me my child has been murdered, but you have questions for me? You know what? It's time for y'all to leave. Get out of my house. You need to be finding the man who killed my baby. That's who you need to be questioning. Get out!"

Ricky snatches the screen door open, and we hurry in, stepping through the vestibule into the living room. Detectives Lee and Dixon are standing up from the deep cushioned brown sofa.

The tip of Ricky's sister's ears have turned beet red along with her cheeks and neck. Brenda is a short woman of wide stature. She is standing in her hospital green housecoat and black sweat pants with her arm offering the Detectives the door. She steps by Ricky and me to the door and opens the screen door.

"I mean now, right now! Leave!"

The detectives walk by Ricky and me without a word. Once they clear the doorjamb, Brenda slams the heavy wooden door shut.

She collapses to her knees with the bang of the door.

"Sweet Jesus, Babygirl, not you, please Lord not my child, not my baby." She cries in a whisper.

Ricky goes to her. I take a half a step toward them and then a half a step back. The area is too small for me to join them.

Too many of our youth have met with death. Too many parents have fallen to their knees. Too many family futures have been wrecked by the death of their children. Too many of our babies are dying. And I'm sick of it. I turn away, walk into the dining room, and sit at the table.

Nothing can be said to relieve a parent's suffering grief. The pain of a lost child is without equal. Not a word said to me made me feel any better. No prayer soothed my heart. An hour didn't pass when I didn't think of my son. It wasn't until the birth of my second son did the hands of woe ease its constant grip on my heart and mind.

"What am I gonna do?" Brenda wails from the vestibule, "How can I tell Reynard Babygirl is dead? Lord that will kill him. He loves his child. Oh Lord he loves her. What we gonna do Ricky? What we gonna do?"

He doesn't answer her. How could he?

I lower my head and do the only thing I can think to do, pray. I'm not one to pray with people because my prayers are brief, quick talks with God. Right now, I ask Him to comfort this family, to ease some of the pain and to give them strength to endure the unendurable, and I pray that she and her husband stay together and not blame each other.

I open my eyes because the air of someone passing me breezes over my shaved head. It's Brenda going to the bathroom. I say amen to end the prayer. I have no words for her, but it occurs to me that there is something I can do.

These murders are happening on my streets. Streets where I am acquainted with folks. Streets were people respect and care about me. He murdered in my neighborhood. My knowledge of the area is better than the police and the people or places I am not familiar with Ricky or my brother will be. I can find the bastard that killed this child. That's what I can do. That's within my reach.

I feel the correctness of the decision all through me. It's like that for me when I'm doing something right, something unselfish. A brother tingles a bit. Mostly around the ears, and right now I am tingling from the mere thought of finding this sick fuck. I rise from the armed dining chair and walk back to the living-room.

I find Ricky on the floor in the small vestibule struggling to get up. He tries to elevate himself using one leg with his back against the door, but he slides back down to the floor. Then he tries with both legs but has no success. He rocks, he twists, he turns, but nothing helps. He is unable to rise.

This is not a time to laugh. The man just lost his niece . . . but . . . it is a funny sight. This huge yellow brother squirming around on the hardwood floor of the small vestibule with his green gator shoes kicking around trying to find support. His fancy tailor-made green linen pants are of no help. Maybe if he had on jeans he wouldn't be sliding across the wood. What's seen is funny, and I want to laugh, so I bite my lip to stop the chuckle.

He grunts, rolls, and tries again, but it's not going to happen. There is not enough space in the vestibule to allow him to anchor himself. He would have to crawl out to the living-room couch to get up. And he's not going to let me or any man of this earth see him crawling.

What was slight perspiration has grown into a full sweat. The finger waves in his hair are beginning to muss. Strands are rising here and there, and his breathing is labored and loud.

It has to be said, and I have to say it.

"Help me, I have fallen, and I can't get up."

He looks up at me, grunts, blows a heavy breath, and starts laughing.

"Fuck you awight, this here situation ain't funny. I need some help. Give me yo' damn hand man."

With my eyes watering, I extend my hand and try to help him up, but he's too much for one hand and arm. I offer him both. I hoist, he rocks forward, farts, and rises.

On his feet he catches his breath, and pulls a handkerchief from his hip pocket, and pats his forehead dry. Well, almost dry.

He says, "I called and got a trainer out at da health club on 95th Street. I start dis evening, so I ain't gon' be da brunt of too many more of dese kind of jokes, partner. I'ma get dis fat off of me."

He bumps past me to the dining room.

I quickly exit to the porch to laugh out loud. My daddy, a devout Catholic, has always told me I would laugh at a dead Pope, and I probably would if something funny happened at the funeral.

On the porch, I unbutton the top button of my thin black leather jacket, and reach into the inside pocket and retrieve my phone to dial the office. Carol, my partner and office manager, is not going to be happy about my absence from the office this morning. We have a training class starting today, and me not being there doesn't look very professional.

Image is paramount with Carol. She is a conservative, almost puritan dresser with an all business persona in the office. I would not have hired this present Carol as an assistant. She has developed into this austere partner largely due to my lackadaisical operational attitude. I like the job not the paper work. She took to the managerial aspects of the company like jackleg preacher to tithes and offerings.

"Hello. Epsilon Security Services. May I help you?"

"Hey, Carol, it's me."

"Oh God, David. I heard about Ricky's niece. I have rescheduled your orientations for the next few days. Keith will fill in for most of them. How are Ricky and the girl's parents?"

How did she find out already, the news? No, not yet. It had to be my ex-wife looking for info.

"Regina called you?"

31

"Yes, she said she tried to reach you but you didn't answer your phone."

"Huh? We were just together. What did she ask you for?"

"Ricky's sister's phone number and address I looked through your rolodex contacts and gave it to her. Was that ok?"

"No problem."

What would it have hurt Regina to ask me for the information instead going around me? Why is being direct such a problem for that woman?

"Carol, I am going to need a little time with this today. Plan on seeing me after five; can you stay until six or so?"

"Yes, of course."

"Cool."

"You be smart, boss. Think with your head first, do not get committed to doing the police department's job. They are capable of finding this murderer."

"Damn, girl, you starting to know me too good."

"Not good but well. I know you well."

"Good, well, whatever, you got my meaning."

"Yes, I get your meaning. Are you okay with Keith filling in for the training?"

"Oh yeah, good choice, he watched me do enough of them. Okay then, I'll see you tonight and thanks again."

"See you this evening."

I flip the phone closed. Stepping to the edge of the porch I take a deep head-clearing breath. The air chills the back of my throat. I got to get Ricky on board with the idea of looking for the murderer, but that shouldn't be too hard. Babygirl was his blood.

The problem is going to be once we find the murderer. Getting the killer to the police instead of the grave will be a challenge. Ricky kills about his family. I flip my phone open again and push in Regina's numbers.

"Hey, Gina, it's David."

"Hey, sweetie," she answers.

Sweetie? My ex-wife hasn't called me 'sweetie' since early in our marriage, and if memory serves me correctly the lovable name only came before a request, usually something she was uncomfortable asking.

"Hey there yourself, gorgeous."

'Gorgeous' was my name for her when sex was on my mind. Since she wants to play, let us play.

"Mmph, haven't heard you call me that in sometime . . . a very long time actually."

"Yes, but seldom spoken doesn't mean seldom thought."

"You been thinking about calling me gorgeous but haven't done it?"

"Slim, there are a lot of things I been thinking about in regards to you and haven't done."

"Mr. Price, are you mackin' me?"

"I don't think people use that term any more, gorgeous."

"Well then, are you trying to put a move on me, flirt with me, hook up with me. Me, your ex-wife, the mother of your sons."

The mother of my sons; Eric, the one whose death I blamed on her, and Chester, the one she kept secret three years. Am I flirting with this woman? Am I trying to mack her?

Why not? I have learned that time heals most wounds, and the truth of the matter is she looked damn good to me this morning.

"And if I was slightly mackin'?"

"I would be flattered, extremely flattered."

"I don't see why. It's like I always told you, you the finest woman God ever let walk this earth."

I believed that to be the pure truth when I first told it to her over thirteen years ago, and I still believe it.

"You need to stop."

"Why?"

"Cause . . . you called me for a reason, D. What was it?"

I called to set her straight about going around me for information, but it appears something else might be brewing. But a smart brother can't help but wonder who is doing the brewing or the mackin'. She did start it all with calling me 'sweetie.'

"I called because I need to stop by your place tonight about nine thirty or so."

She gets sleepy early. Add a little wine and a little more mackin', who knows what might happen.

"Why do you want to come by?"

Why do I want to come by? I should tell her because I want some pussy, bad. Because I dream about being with you and my son as a family at least once a week, because a man like me needs a woman to complete his life, and because at one time you were that woman and maybe you could be again, because I am accustomed to your flaws and now think I could live with them, and because I am lonely and horny as hell. That's why.

But what I say is, "Got something I need to talk to you about. I been looking at some downtown real-estate and need your opinion."

"You! Please, I know you're not thinking about leaving Englewood."

She's right I'm not, but, "One never knows," is my reply.

"Make it closer to ten after Chester is asleep."

After Chester is asleep, now that's a good sign.

"See you then."

"Okay, sweetie, see you then." She clicks off.

Again with the sweetie, my mind goes to her looking at my jones this morning, her eyes were lingering. Maybe Detective Lee ain't all that, and she is looking to come back home to where she knows it's good. Maybe she is remembering and missing the way we used to get down on the sheets. I know I do. Yeah, she's looking to come home to Daddy.

Wow, I didn't feel it happen but looking down I see I have gotten as hard as a fifteen-year-old looking at his first pair of real tits. Damn, thinking about my ex-wife has me like this. Who woulda thought it? I flip the phone closed as the screen-door opens.

I turn to see Ricky whose face is twisted in disgust.

"Damn! What you out here dialing 1-900 numbers. You kinda old fo' dat shit ain't cha? You need to do somethin' about what's goin' on down there."

He nods toward my crouch.

It's been awhile since I made a tent in my pants. I put my hand in my boxers and pull my jones up putting the head behind my belt buckle. It will go down in a minute.

"I just got off the phone with Regina. We got a date tonight, and, bro, it sounds like we really got a date!"

Ricky lets out an exasperated breath.

"Man, real life goin' on in dis house, and you out here goin' down fantasy lane. Dat woman is finished with you, D, unless she needs

35

somethin' from you. Don't do dat to ya'self. Please don't."

He could be right, but I ain't trying to hear him right now. Later for what he's talking about. He didn't hear the tone of the conversation, or her calling me 'sweetie,' but this is not the time to labor a point with him. My teenage boy desires are ill suited for the present situation, and I know that.

"Yeah you right, man. Let's go back inside, and talk with your sister."

"Nope. Yo' ass needs to stay out here fo' a minute. She don't need to see you all swollen up down dere. Keep your horny ass on da porch until you calm down. Damn. What is you thankin'?"

He goes back inside, and lets the screen door slam behind him.

Man. I am still brick hard, so hard that being behind the belt hurts. I move my jones from under my belt and the tent returns. It must be the pills I took this morning. The ones the herb doctor gave Ricky. They are probably keeping me in this state. My jones is not going down. It's the strangest thing because I don't feel like I'm erect, but I am. This could be a problem.

"Hey!"

At the foot of the porch on the sidewalk is a dusty, skinny, bag lady looking woman with nicotine stained teeth.

"I can take care of that for you."

She puckers her chapped flakey lips and blows a kiss toward my jones.

"All you got to do is buy me a pint of wine and a crack-rock. I got the best head on the Southside, and I swallow, and if I don't get you off with my mouth you can have some pussy," she says with a wink.

It is fall, and most of the summer flies are dead, but somehow she manages to have two or three buzzing around her. She opens her tattered, grimy red flannel jacket, and flashes me with her flat, weathered, and it looks like dried mustard stained breast.

"I can take care of you right there in the gangway," she says nodding her towards the space between the two brick homes.

Ricky's pills are no match for what my eyes are witnessing. My jones deflates. I reach into my pocket, and peel a ten from my bankroll because she did take care of the problem. She's up the stairs before I can extend the bill to her.

"You want me to do you right here on the porch?"

"No! Just take the money and go."

A pissy musty odor came up the stairs with her.

"I ain't got a problem with doing you right here."

"I believe you, but that's not needed, take this ten and go-head-on. Matter of fact . . . here," I peel a twenty from my roll, "take this and get something to eat."

She snatches both bills and flees the porch.

"Your chances were better with her dan Regina," Ricky says from behind the screen door.

I turn to see his whole face grinning at me, fat bastard. There is nothing funny about what just happened or what he just said, but he's laughing like a hyena.

*

When I go back into the house, I tell Brenda that I will try to find her daughter's killer. Ricky promises we will. Convincing him to join in the investigation is a moot point. He is in as soon as I mention to Brenda about looking into the case. I reiterate to both of them that my professional title is that of a Personal Escort, not a detective, but they will get my best effort.

Ricky is anxious to get started; he all but runs from his sister's house to my car once his wife Martha and some neighbors arrive.

"We should get on it right away befo' the murderer finds out it's more than the police lookin' fo' him. We need to find out as much as we can before da streets start talkin' about us being involved."

His point is valid, so started we are.

Chapter Five

In the car, I have to sit for a minute. Ricky's rush can't be mine. Proceeding with the investigation must be done at my pace, so that I can think and formulate a plan of action. Moving at Ricky's or anyone else's speed will lead me to errors and redoing. So I am deliberately slowing the pace down.

"What we have to do first, is to find a common link between the girls."

I start the car and pause to put on my seatbelt and wait for Ricky to fasten his. The city has started this 'click it or ticket' mess, and the fine is significant. He huffs but pulls the belt across.

"They all Black and live n da 'hood. Dat's da common link."

"That's true, but we need something more, something more detailed, more specific."

"Like what?"

I'm not sure how to say this to him. I identified a possible link from Brenda's outburst toward the detectives. She was upset saying it, so the possible link may not be a comfortable topic for the family.

"I heard Brenda tell the police that Babygirl was using drugs."

I pull onto the street.

"So?"

"Robert said two of the girls that died had gotten high with him before. They were drug users. That's a common thread."

"Shit, I don't know how specific dat is dese here days. Damn near everybody is a drug user."

We need to stop by the office first so I can update Carol face to face on my involvement in the case. She won't be happy about it.

"That's not true, Ricky, and you know it, and don't do that."

"Don't do what?"

He's slipping the seat belt behind him still fastened.

"Don't down our whole community because of the actions of a few. We have more people in church than smoking crack. More of our young men are in school than selling cocaine rocks. More of our young women are working rather than hoein'.

"When we generalize badly about ourselves we are self inflicting negative thoughts and self prophesying. If we are constantly putting our community down verbally, we are hurting the whole by speaking into existence the negative. 'Everybody using drugs'. Not everybody in the community is using drugs, and please don't down us like that."

I make a left onto Halsted. Might as well take it up to 87th Street.

"Nigga what?" Ricky rolls down his window and hacks up and out a glob of spit. I'm glad the glob cleared my window and the car. I roll my window a bit as well because my big friend does generate heat, and the car is getting a little warm.

"Everybody is smokin' dat shit, yo brother, my niece, every fool on da corner either sellin' it or smokin' it. Hell we ain't got to speak it into existence da shit got us by da throat. Damn near every family got two or three crack-heads. You need to wake da fuck up and realize how things is out here."

He rolls his window halfway up.

"It's people like you actin' like 'oh it ain't dat bad' dats really da problem. Shit is dat bad! Now let's fix it! Dat's how mothefuckers gotta start thinkin'. Let's fix some shit. Fuck 'inflicting negative thought'. Motherfuckers need to open up some halfway houses. Get some job programs started fo' young ass niggas. Shit we need some government spendin' not positive thinkin'.

"Some federally funded summer jobs and paid youth trainin' programs. See, you motherfuckers sayin' it ain't dat bad, ain't demandin' shit from da government. Da motherfuckin' military should not be da only option for a Black kid not college bound. Man, don't come to me about speakin' some shit into existence. We need to change some shit dat is existin'.

"Damn you got my motherfucking head hurtin' with dat stupid shit. I need somethin' to eat fo' real. Let's go to Izola's."

He's got to be kidding. He just called me stupid eight different ways, and now he thinks I'm taking his fat ass to a restaurant. Maybe working with him on this is not such a good idea.

"I'm too stupid of a motherfucker to drive to Izola's partner. And ain't a thing on her menu that a man in your physical condition should eat."

Yeah, I went there and fuck him, so what, calling me stupid.

He grunts and sits up as best he can considering his girth.

"Look-a-here man, you started dis sayin' I was self prophesyin' negative shit on Black people. How you gonna say somethin' like dat but get all touchy when a man defends himself? What, you can throw a punch but can't take one?

"Was my argument dat much better den yours? I mean you da one dat graduated from college and all. Yours shoulda been better. I know you ain't upset because a ignorant Southside boy like me made a better point."

"We went to the same school, Ricky."

"Yeah, but you graduated."

"Your point wasn't better. Perhaps I over simplified mine, but what

I said is true."

"Yeah but what I said made mo' sense. Let's go to Izola's. She got salads."

He is not going to order a salad from Izola's. Soul Food is served there. No way he's gonna see food like broiled pork chops, fried corn, cabbage and peppers, catfish steaks, beets in sweet sauce, mustard and turnip greens, and order a salad. Maybe a plate of potato salad with salmon croquets.

"I gotta stop by the office first, and after that we should go up to the center and talk to Robert for a minute. He has lived within the community of drug users for years. If anyone can give us a starting point it's him."

We stop at a red light on 79th and Halsted. It's a busy pedestrian intersection. People are out on all four corners. Most are moving and going about the business of an afternoon, but some are posted against store walls and light poles. A couple of the young men could be drug dealers; however, no obvious drug dealing is seen. The corners are not bubbling with addicts and dealers.

Ok . . . I do see one kid on a bike selling something to a guy standing in the drug store parking lot. Another lady is following a young man into the doorway of a boarded up store. He hands her something, and she hands him something. They could be exchanging phone numbers.

The light turns green and we move on.

"What about Izola's?"

Ricky thumbs a left. I keep straight.

"The office, Robert, then Izola's. Ok?"

"Cool."

"What time do you meet your new personal trainer?"

"Why?"

"'Cause, I want to make sure it's still on your mind with everything that's happening around us that's all."

"I meet da guy at 5:45 up derc on 95th Street. Da gym is way west past Western Avenue. The trainer is one of Martha's friend's husband. He's supposed to be pretty good. He trains some of da Bulls and a couple of da Bears."

I'm halfway expecting him to blow the appointment off. Get involved with finding Claire's killer and toss the weight loss aside.

"Did Brenda reach Reynard?"

"Yeah while you was on the porch. He should be dere by now. Dat house is gonna bc sad for a minute. Dey loved dat girl wid all dey had. Babygirl was dat man's heart."

His voice wavers and he turns his head to look out thc window.

Ricky loved her, too.

*

We walk in the office, and I am surprised by Carol sitting alone behind her thin black lacquer desk. She waves hello by twiddling her thin fingers. She's on the phone. Based on the number of cars parked out front, the office should be full of folks.

I sit in the chair behind my not as chic school teacher's desk, and Ricky drops into the chair in front of my desk. Three pink message pad notes are on my desk. One call is from my brother Robert's social worker, Ms. Flowers, a very nice looking woman with an hour glass shape and a honey colored complexion and a sweet disposition. She wants a call back ASAP. She will get that. A call from Robert also from the center, and he too wants a call back ASAP as well, and a call from the BMW salesman. The '03s are in. I'm gonna have to go see those.

"Hey, D and Mr. Brown. Mr. Brown I am sorry about your loss." Carol rises from her little swivel chair and comes over and gives Ricky a hug. This is a first. She usually won't touch Ricky because of his shameless flirting.

"You and your family are in my prayers."

"Thank you," is his quiet mumble.

She stands erect from the embrace and looks to me, "I have to go upstairs and check on the training. Can you join me?"

The woman is looking very professional in her tan two piece skirt suit with high collar pink blouse. She looks like the owner of this personal security firm. Me, in my tailor made black pants and leather jacket and black alligator shoes . . . at best I look like an applicant or prospective client.

"No, I'm going to return these," holding up the pink squares, "and then leave. Just came to tell you that you do know me well, and I'm going to need a couple of days away from the office."

Shaking her head from side to side causing the short curls in her hair to dance a bit, she says, "We can't stand more than five. We can struggle through the classroom training without you, but only you can lead the field training. It's the law."

Her slanted eyes are on me hard. I nod yes and say, "It won't be more than three, I promise."

Ricky opens his eyes a bit wider because he rarely hears me promise anything.

"Ok," she answers, "I'm going upstairs. Call me, D, a lot. Keep me in the loop."

She turns her thin petite frame and proceeds out the door. I push the speaker function on the phone and dial the health center's number from the social worker's message.

"Sandi Flowers, how can I help you?"

"Hey, Ms. Flowers, this is David Price, Robert Price's brother."

"Good day, Mr. Price, thanks for returning my call."

Pap! Pap! Pap!

"Oh my God, they are shooting! They're shooting! Oh Jesus, Lord have mercy."

"Hello! Hey! Hello!"

No answer. The line clicks dead.

"Damn, man, we got to go! Did you hear that? It sounds like somebody is shooting up the health center!"

Chapter Six

We get here in less than ten minutes. No police yet. People are fleeing from the health center's double-doors. The center sits facing Sixty-Ninth Street on Laflin. I park directly in front of the one story building, and barely get the car in park before Ricky opens his door and struggles out.

No one is stopping to answer any questions, and Ricky and I are the only people moving toward the center. A guy in blue scrubs is holding one of the double-doors open allowing a line of yelling kids out. I follow Ricky through the other side of the double-door. We hear no shots, only screams.

In the lobby behind the reception desk is the security guard. He has been rocked back in the office chair, and his forehead has been opened. I count three blood leaking wounds. No need to go to him. I draw one of my pistols. Ricky's is already in his hand.

Behind the reception desk is the lobby seating area. People are running through the orange and blue plastic chairs trying to get to the double-doors behind us. There are three corridors beyond the seating area. Seniors are emerging from the one to the left, and kids and more grown folks are running from the one to the right. Down the center corridor is where the outpatient drug treatment program is housed. Ms. Flower's office is down that hall, and so are Robert and Nikki.

"Center hall, man," I tell Ricky as we pass through the chairs.

We see the kid at the same time.

He sees us, and stops.

We stop, too, and so do the old people and the children. They stop moving and screaming. The waiting area is hushed. Everybody sees him. He has a pistol in each hand. He walks to the center of the waiting area about five steps away from me and Ricky, and stops.

"I told his white ass to leave her alone. I told him to stop giving her that shit, but he kept doing it. So I blew his motherfuckin' brains out!" he tells Ricky, "I ain't no fuckin' joke. He shoulda asked somebody. He was keeping her sicker than the crack-rocks and the heroin. A doctor is supposed to help people. That motherfucker was just trying to keep his dick wet with Black pussy. Fuck him!"

All the while he is speaking his eyes are on Ricky. The kid rolls his shoulders and stretches his neck to the left until it pops. He does the same to the right, and smiles a little from the relief of the neck stretch and pop.

"I ain't crazy. I wouldna shot the guard except for he tried to flex like he had some authority. I came up here for the doctor. My girl overdosed on that stuff he gave her last night. She's dead, so his ass had to die.

"Now, if y'all ain't the police, you best be gettin' the fuck outta my way. I'm done here."

Ricky steps aside, and so do I.

The kid walks by us and out the double-doors. If someone was to ask me right now what clothes he had on I couldn't say, but I could tell them he had a black Desert Eagle .9mm in his left hand and a silver Smith and Wesson .357 in his right.

And as if somebody flipped a switch, the screams start again and people go back to running from the heath center. I move toward the center corridor.

In the hall, I see Ms. Flowers on the floor of the hallway bent over a man in a doctor's smock.

48

The kid was accurate in his words. The doctor's brains are splattered against the white wall and dripping down to the black baseboard. The kid had to have hollow points in the .357 to spread the doctor's brain over that much wall.

The pretty Ms. Flowers nor anyone else on this earth can do a thing for the doctor, but she is on her knees with him mumbling and praying. I reach down to her shoulder and shake her. When she looks up at me, it is clear that she is not here. Her almost black eyes are unfocused. I bend down and pull her up and away from the corpse.

*

Outside of the health center she is refusing to get into the ambulance.

"There is absolutely nothing wrong with me. You people need to go and tend to those seniors over there against the wall."

She points her manicured finger to a group of seniors standing in the grass using the center's brick wall for support.

She is right. The old people are obviously in need of care. The attendants roll the wheelchairs in their direction.

Once again, I am in the midst of press, police, and paramedics. Ms. Flowers slides her navy suit jacket back on and adjusts her long hair from beneath it.

"Mr. Price I can't thank you enough for your concern and aid. All I remember is talking to you on the phone and then hearing the shots. The next thing I recall is standing out here in the sun with you holding me. I'm aware the shooting happened, but it's not in my mind, and I'm thankful for that."

She pauses, and I watch her round brown eyes peruse the crowd. She was still dazed when the morgue people removed the doctor's and the guard's bodies. She only became alert after a paramedic snapped a tube of something under her nose.

"My God, Dr. Aims. His death will destroy his poor wife."

I want to ask her about what the kid shooter accused Dr. Aims of, but I see tears forming in her eyes. This isn't the time. The detectives have been biding their time as well waiting patiently off to the side to talk to her. They have ignored Ricky and me for the most part, and I want to keep it that way.

"D!"

It's my bother calling me from the corner. He's with Ricky and Nikki.

"Go to your brother, Mr. Price. I have duties waiting for me inside the clinic." She rises up on her tip toes and kisses me on the cheek, "Thank you again."

She turns and walks up the concrete sidewalk to the waiting detectives and through the double-doors.

"D!" my brother yells again. I turn from her to him. He is almost jumping up and down on the corner.

When I get to them he says, "I knew Claire, man! Me and Nikki both knew her, and we know the dude she was staying with. But I didn't know she was your niece, man," he says turning his head from me to Ricky. "I just didn't remember her like that. I met her on the streets, man, doing what we do."

He shrugs his shoulders and takes a couple half steps to the left and the right. He does this when he is uncomfortable, and I guess his not recognizing Claire got him a little guilty.

"I gotcha, man, I understand, but you say you know where she was stayin'?" Ricky asks.

"Yeah, she was with Ole Jumpy. He lets girls stay with him all the time. He got a house on Bishop, sixty-eight seventeen. His mama left it to him a couple of years ago. He rents rooms . . . mostly to young chicks. He lets some stay for free. Well, not free, but you know what I mean." His eyes dart down the block away from Ricky. He didn't mean to say that.

"Nikki used to stay there sometimes. I can take y'all over there right now and get back before things settle down around here. Because Ms. Flowers ain't gonna close the center, we still gonna have evening group, you can bet on that."

"You kidding?" me and Ricky ask.

"Umph," Nikki says, "No, he ain't . . . . Ms. Flowers will have group the day Jesus comes back. She bills the state for every group, and she ain't 'bout to miss no money. Her and Dr. Aims is death on them dollars. Oh . . . he was death on them dollars until death came calling."

She and Robert burst out laughing and lean into each other. They think what she just said is funny. They laugh all the way back to my car. But the laughter becomes suspect because it's nervous laughter. Edgy laughter, quick bird-like chirps of laughter. I have heard this type of laughter from my brother before. He laughs this way when he is trying to hide the fact that he is high.

I pause on the sidewalk and take a step back and look at them; they are animated in their movements and speech and straining to appear sober and normal.

I step to my brother and grab him by the shoulder and spin him around.

"Yo' ass is high!"

He starts to say something, but stops.

51

He lowers his head and says, "Hey, you got the address. Ole Jumpy will talk to y'all. We going back in the center."

Neither he nor she will look at me as they walk past. I hit the tab on my keypad unlocking the BMW's doors. I don't even watch them walk away. I go into the street, open the driver's door and get into my car.

"This nigga!" I say slamming my car door closed.

Chapter Seven

Because of a scheduled street sweeping we had to park down the block from Ole Jumpy's address. The sunny morning has turned to late afternoon, and the last of the morning's sun is tinting the city's sky amber.

This is a nice block. All the houses are occupied and people seem to care enough to keep up their lawns and keep trash off the block.

We are walking past a mixture of frame houses and raised ranch homes. We used to call the raised ranch models the 'new houses' because when we were kids they were building them throughout the 'hood. Now families have been raised in them, maybe even two generations. I guess they ain't the 'new houses' any more.

Across the street a group of kids are engaged in a vigorous game of Red Light, Green Light. A couple of them are in their blue checkered uniform skirts and navy-blue school pants. They are taking advantage of the last clear weather play days.

When we get to sixty-eight seventeen, the atmosphere around the old frame house is different from the rest of the block. It's obvious by the trimmed lawns, the swept curbs, and maintained houses that people of this block care about their property. The look of sixty-eight seventeen doesn't relay that feeling. Its small lawn is patchy and sparse with a few clumps of weeds and grass sprouting up through the hard pressed dirt.

The poorly kept lawn is encased by a wooden plank fence. The few remaining planks of the fence are splintered with age and are badly in need of a coat of paint. The whole house needs painting, bad. The beige paint that once covered it is flaked and weathered. The bottom step and a middle step are missing from the stairs that lead to the porch. The right handrail is beyond slack, and is barely attached to the frame house.

We don't have to knock when we get up on the porch because the door is flung open by a young woman fleeing. A barefoot, potbellied man in blue jean shorts and a khaki work shirt is chasing her. Ricky extends his foot tripping the skinny man with a pot gut, aiding in the young lady's freedom.

The fallen man at our feet has hair as sparse as the lawn, and he is missing as many teeth as the front fence is planks.

"Who the fuck tripped me?" he asks from his knees on the porch.

"Dat was my mistake. Didn't see you comin'," Ricky offers the man a hand up. He saw the man, but Ricky always helps the woman in a fight.

"Jumpy?" Ricky asks the man while helping him up.

"Yeah I'm Jumpy . . . hold up . . . I know you," he says standing. "You Ricky Brown! I use to gamble at your spot off of Cicero and Lake street, and the one Eighty-third and Ashland. I followed the Ashland game to Forty-ninth and Wentworth, but after that I fell off. I got into other stuff."

From the curb, the girl he chased from the house says, "I hope you broke your old ass neck!"

Jumpy flinches as if he's going to run after her but thinks better of it.

"Come on chase me," the girl yells from the curb, "and have a fucking stroke! Come get me, old man!"

Jumpy is trying to ignore her heckling. To me and Ricky he says, "Ricky Brown on my porch, ain't that something."

54

Ricky used to host floating dice games all over the city. That enterprise along with owning the majority of the liquor stores on the Southside, and his apartment buildings, and he and Martha's cleaning service, and various other semi-legal and illegal activities gets him celebrity status in the 'hood.

Nodding his head, Ricky snaps his fingers and says, "Oh yeah, I remember you. You shoot left handed and like to bet da bar, six and eights. You hit fo' close to eight grand one night out west."

Ole Jumpy is standing and offering a missing-teeth grin to Ricky, "Seventy-six hundred! Sho' did," he says pridefully. "That was the best night of my life."

Ricky doesn't return Jumpy's cheerful mood. His face is stern. He is almost mean-mugging Ole Jumpy. He says, "But people didn't call you Jumpy back den."

Jumpy's face fidgets with blinking eyes and twitching lips. He lowers his head avoiding Ricky's probing eyes. He dusts off his blue jean shorts and answers, "Naw, they didn't. My name is Neal, Neal Henson. This Ole Jumpy shit started recently. I'm high-strung by nature, mix that with other stuff and you get a jumpy person. So they started calling me Jumpy, then Ole Jumpy. I can't shake the name, so Ole Jumpy I am."

The girl who ran from the house is in the middle of the street yelling, "Hey, old man!" she screams. "And I still ain't paying you shit! Pussy ain't free, even if you can't fuck it. You pay to lick it. And If I ever see ya ass again . . . it will be too soon."

She then pulls her grey sweat pants down and points her ashy ass at him. She smacks her left butt cheek with her left palm and flicks her wrist and fingers into the universal 'Fuck You' sign. She yanks up her sweat pants and runs down the block.

That totally trips out the kids across the street. The group bursts open in laughter.

Ole Jumpy says, "That little slut been staying here for two months free. She got her Social Security settlement check a couple of days ago and refused to give me a dime." He watches her sprint around the corner, "She'll be back when the money runs out, and then she will be singing a different song. Winter coming, too. Oh yeah, she'll be back."

Ricky and I look at each other but say nothing. It's obvious that Ole Jumpy is a man who benefits from other's misfortune, particularly young women. If it was just about the money, making a profit from renting rooms, I could understand. But it ain't like that with him. He is preying on young homeless women based on their need for housing. His help is offered in exchange for sex, and that's just plain pitiful.

That means he has no game at all, none. No other way of obtaining female companionship except through commerce, and for the exchange to involve younger, more naive women speaks further to his weakness as a man. And the sad part is that the 'hood is full of parasites just like him, and women who need to play their weak game.

"Hey, Neal or Jumpy, we here to ask you about a girl named Claire. She was stayin' wid you, right?"

I wouldn't have been as direct, but Ricky has taken the lead.

"Oh yeah, she was staying here, a pretty young thing with some good ass pussy. Her stuff was tighter than Dick's hat band. She wouldn't give head though, threw up when I tried to make her."

I don't see it happen, but Ricky hits the man so hard and so fast that all I see are his feet sailing by me. He flies from the porch to the sidewalk leading to his tattered steps. He hits the concrete with a thud and a crack. I think his shoulder broke.

Ricky goes down the steps in one motion, and his huge frame is atop Ole Jumpy. He forces his pistol into the man's gasping-for-breath mouth and tells him to, "Suck on dis, motherfucker. Suck it like yo' life depends on it, cause it does. Suck it. She was my blood, nigga, and yo' hands shouldna touched her!"

I go down the stairs knowing there is nothing I can do to help Ole Jumpy. He's trying to talk but Ricky has the whole barrel of his .45 in the man's mouth. Ole Jumpy is squirming like an earthworm under Ricky's girth.

I look to the front door, but no one has come from the house. The kids from across the street are now standing on the curb watching the action.

Ricky withdraws the pistol from Jumpy's mouth. He lifts it above his head and brings the butt of it down on Ole Jumpy's eye.

"Agh!" Jumpy screams, "Please, man I didn't know. Don't kill me, Mr. Brown. Please, don't kill me. She came here like all the others looking for a place to stay. I didn't know she was your family, man. I swear to God I didn't know!"

Ricky hits him in the eye again with the pistol butt.

"He got a gun!" One of the kids across the street scream, and I see all of them scatter away from the curb.

Ricky brings the pistol down for another blow.

"The doctor took her from me, man!" Ole Jumpy yells, "She left a couple of days ago to stay in his house. She's staying with him!"

"What doctor?" Ricky growls.

"The one who runs the treatment clinic on Sixty-Ninth Street, he got her, Mr. Brown. I ain't got her. He knows where she is."

Ricky stands with surprising ease and kicks the man square in the balls with his green alligator shoes. I flinch from the pain I am certain Ole Jumpy is experiencing.

"Clean up yo' fuckin' act. You damn pervert."

Then he stomps on Jumpy's shoulder. The one I am sure he broke in the fall. Ole Jumpy's pitiful screaming could make a dead rat's tail curl. Ricky is standing over the man with the gun still in his hand. I can see that he wants to shoot Ole Jumpy, bad.

Ole Jumpy must be able to see it too because he says, "Agh! Jesus please, please, please don't kill me, Mr. Brown. Please don't," he cries.

I step right up on my best friend. Getting in his face I say, "He didn't kill her, Ricky."

"Yeah, but he took her low."

"But he didn't kill her."

Ricky is patting his thigh with the pistol, thinking.

Ole Jumpy stares up at Ricky, and then me, knowing his life is being tossed around in Ricky's mind. His eyes rest on the pistol tapping Ricky's thigh.

"Please, Mr. Brown," he begs.

Ricky huffs, and hacks up a knot of mucus and splats it on Ole Jumpy's forehead. He puts his pistol under his sweater. He turns from Ole Jumpy and me, and he walks through the matted dirt lawn, and raggedy fence. He doesn't use the gate. He walks through the plank fence destroying what's left of it.

*

In the car he says, "Dat damn doctor was a twisted motherfucker. I bet we gonna find out dat all da dead girls was his patients. We need to go through his records."

I'm thinking the same thing. There is definitely more to the doctor than him being a victim.

"We need to go back up to da clinic and make dat social worker open up her files."

He rolls down the passenger window and spits into the street. I think about the glob he left on Ole Jumpy's forehead and smile.

"Dat's da next move. We got to make her ass give up dem files."

I agree, but that won't happen with Ricky present. His anger will close doors. Things need to move at my pace, not Ricky's, and in his company, we will continue to snowball through on emotion. I have learned that emotions cloud facts. It is time to get rid of Ricky. I look at my Rolex and see it's five forty-five.

"What time is your gym appointment?"

"That can wait. Let's get up to the health center."

"No, the appointment can't wait. I can handle Ms. Flowers. You need to handle your health. All of this can't be good for your heart."

"Let me worry about my health, we onto somethin' here."

"We are onto something, true enough, but it's not going to change between now and tomorrow morning. Life is more than one thing, one situation. We're going to find the killer together, but we both got other responsibilities in our lives. I am taking you home, but I will be at your door at eight o'clock tomorrow morning."

"What time da center open?"

"Ms. Flowers gets there at nine."

"Awight den. I guess you makin' sense. You know I ain't ate shit since we started, so I am workin' on my health, too. Hey, pull into dat Burger King drive-thru," he orders. "With Martha over my sister's I know ain't nothin' at home to eat."

"Are you getting a salad?"

59

"Fuck you, a Double Whopper . . . but only one instead of three."

*

Once I get to the crib after dropping Ricky off, I realize how bad I need to unplug from him, the murders, and my crack smoking brother. But unplugging ain't possible.

The yellow police tape behind my house won't let me unplug from the murders, and my brother not being home won't let me unplug from him, and thinking about the murders gets me to thinking about Claire which puts Ricky right back on my mind.

Sitting on my couch, I take out my phone and call up to the center for Ms. Flowers. She doesn't have a problem meeting with me after group. Matter of fact, she says she was about to call me to discuss my brother's living arrangement. It seems he told her he is now homeless and needs to stay in their men's shelter. I assure her that my brother has a place to stay and agree that a meeting is needed.

As soon as I click my cell phone off from Ms. Flowers, my mother calls on my house phone asking to speak to Robert. She says he is on her mind, and she is just checking to make sure things are ok. She tells me how proud she is that we were working on his problem like a family and how important it is for grown children to be there for one another.

She tells me my brother, Charles, is on his way out to Arizona to spend time with her and my father. She then asks when are me and Robert coming out there to see them. I tell her we will both be out there before Christmas, and I hear the joy that brings to her voice.

She says my daddy has really gotten into golf and is playing four days a week and two of those days she plays too, but most of her time is taken up by the bridge club and the church they joined out there. She says it is really funny watching my daddy with his new white friends.

60

Laughing, she says it took that man to get into his seventies to get friendly with white people. She tells me again how proud she is of us working together and then hangs up with an, "I love y'all."

And after talking to my mother, I feel as if I can relax. I kick off my shoes, stretch out on the couch, and let my eyes close.

Chapter Eight

In the dream, it is my ex-wife, Regina, kissing me on my neck. Then her face morphs, and her light complexion darkens into the face of my secretary Carol, then the slender face of Carol rounds into the pretty face of Ms. Flowers. In reality, it is Yang licking me on my neck to let him and Yin out to the yard.

At the back door I hear them galloping around in the dark yard. The darkness makes me check my watch. It is nine o'clock. I have missed the meeting with my brother and Ms. Flowers.

The door bell sounds, and I go to the front door and peep through the peephole. I see the pretty Ms. Flowers and my pug-nosed brother.

*

It's obvious he hasn't told her that he has gotten high. Maybe if he tells her he has gotten high, she might kick him out of the outpatient program. I don't want that, so I decide not to bring up his getting high in her presence. The point of this meeting seems to be for Ms. Flowers to smooth things out between my brother and me.

I am sitting in the armchair, and she and my bother are on the couch, and the coffee table is between us.

He is sober now, and hasn't said a thing besides hello.

Ms. Flowers adjust her seat on the couch and crosses her legs at the ankles. She is stretching her shapely nylon covered appendages away from her body. She is wearing the same navy blue two piece skirt suit from earlier. I can see the day's weariness in the slack of her face, and fatigue in the droop of her shoulders. She obviously hasn't had a good break all day.

"Mr. Price, we at the center feel that a family environment is better for the recovery process. Especially if the home is drug-free. Our shelter is concerned with only housing. We allow any homeless person to stay there including those that may be still using drugs."

Looking at my brother, thinking about my mother, but speaking to the tired Ms. Flowers, I make up my mind not to drag this out, "There has been a misunderstanding. Robert isn't homeless. He can stay here. As long as he is trying to get clean. I don't expect him to get it perfect, but I do expect him to keep trying."

She pulls her legs in and sits erect on the couch. She looks to me and asks, "Do you have doubts about Robert's sobriety?"

I look straight into her round, brown eyes and say, "Not a doubt in the world," because I am certain the motherfucker got high. But there is no sense in putting her through a thing, or getting Robert further off track.

"My brother is always welcome in my home. He knows that."

Robert looks down at the coffee table avoiding my stare.

"Well good, because I really didn't want to see him in the shelter." She stands, and so do I.

While walking her to the door I ask, "Do you have a minute to talk? I am hearing some strange things about the late Dr. Aims."

She looks back towards my brother and whispers, "On the porch, please."

Outside leaning against a porch post I tell her, "Today I heard two people complain about Dr. Aims being sexually inappropriate with female clients. Three, if I count the kid that shot him. "

She fumbles with car keys while standing on the edge of the porch.

"Lies," she replies. "If not lies, fantasies. You see, a lot of the young women were attached to him. He was a good looking man, and for

64

many of them the only gentle and kind male in their lives.

"Fantasies and crushes developed all the time. He was a healer, Mr. Price, and some of the young ladies took his bedside manner and easy ways for flirtations. I assure you there was nothing going on between him and any patient."

The way she said patient makes me ask, "What about staff?"

"Not to my knowledge. The man loved his wife."

I think about what Ole Jumpy said, and Nikki's confession to Robert and say, "I heard he traded prescription drugs for sexual favors."

She looks by me to the blinking motion detector light on my neighbor Fred's porch. The light is trying to cut itself on due to us being on my porch. I don't have a motion detector. My porch light flips on from the inside. I didn't turn it on, so we are standing in the darkness of the night.

"That's not true. Those same allegations occurred at the Westside clinic, but they were proven false. I worked with Dr. Aims on the Westside. If I had any doubts, I would not have asked him to come out here with me. He was a dedicated professional, Mr. Price."

Fred's light has clicked on illuminating half of my porch in a blue hue. In the light, the fatigue on her face looks hard, almost stern. There is little left of the damsel from this afternoon.

"The young man that killed him seemed certain of his inappropriateness."

She pulls her long hair from beneath her suit jacket and places it over her shoulder. Her glance goes up to the sky. Due to the light pollution of the city, only the North Star can be seen.

"The shooting was a random act of violence which happens in our community way too often."

There was nothing random about the young man's actions, but I won't argue the point. Instead, I probe for information.

"There were three girls murdered on the Westside last year. The cases are very similar to the deaths happening around here. Young Black girls were found dead with a black ribbon around their necks. Were you familiar with those girls from the Westside? Did they attend your Westside clinic?"

The questions are a long shot, but if they hit home I will know to target my investigation around the patients and maybe her and the clinic. Looking into the street I see that she has blocked my driveway with her sedan despite the fact that there is more than enough room to park in front of or behind the driveway. She parked right smack in front of the driveway totally blocking it.

Fumbling with her keys again she says, "Yes, those young ladies were all clients of the clinic."

Pay dirt hit. I zone in with, "Were they patients of Dr. Aims?"

She exhales heavily and says, "Dr. Aims saw all the addiction clients."

Mine is the only driveway on the block that leads to an underground garage. People don't park in front of it because of the severe slant down. One could easily slide down the slope. Most people, especially women in heels, wouldn't risk it.

"So they were his patients?"

"Yes, being patients of the clinic made them his patients. But what you are proposing is crazy, Mr. Price. He wouldn't, couldn't have harmed a soul. It just wasn't part of his make up."

Again, I don't argue. I go for the information.

"Was Claire Anderson a patient at your clinic?"

Her audible breath is more of a sigh than the exhaling attitude.

"Yes, she was new. She had only attended a couple of sessions and groups. We had high hopes for her because she wasn't chronic. She was a lot like Dr. Aims' wife, young and sincere in her desire to stop."

"Are you saying Dr. Aims' wife was a patient?"

Keys jiggling, she answers, "Yes. He met her at the Westside clinic."

"But you just said he didn't get involved with the patients?'

"He married her, Mr. Price. I think that speaks to his humanity."

"The other two girls found the weeks before, were they clients at the clinic as well?"

"Yes, and I have told that to police."

"Damn, Ms. Flowers, girls are coming to your clinic for help and they are turning up dead. Somebody's humanity should be in question."

I am staring hard into her profile, but she won't turn to face me. The blue light is causing her jet black hair to shimmer. Black hair on a brown woman has always been attractive to me . . . even more so if the hair is long. I hear her phone vibrating in her purse.

"These young women live at-risk lives, Mr. Price. You know that. It is admittedly a sad coincidence, but it's nothing more than coincidence. I assure you."

What she is saying is bullshit. She ignores the vibrating phone just like I am ignoring her lies.

"I would like to talk to Dr. Aims' wife. Could you give me her contact information?"

"Certainly, come by the clinic in the morning. Good evening." She takes a step down without making eye contact.

There was a little mutual attraction brewing between us, but it's gone now, and we both know it. She turns completely from me, and walks down the stairs to her Volvo. She manages the decline of the slope with no problem. I watch her get into her sedan before I go back in the house.

The pretty Ms. Sandi Flowers has rubbed me the wrong way. She is either in denial or a liar. Coincidence my ass. Somebody in her circle is or was killing girls. A blind, once-a-year-nut-finding squirrel could see that.

When I get into the house, my brother is standing next to the doorway. He was eavesdropping.

"She a damn lie," he snaps into my ear. "Everybody knows Dr. Aims was as crooked as a knotted snake. The people out West ran him and her up out of that clinic.

"They say her ass knows how to write grants, and that's why she keeps getting director jobs. If it wasn't for her, Dr. Aims' ass would have been practicing medicine in Bum Fuck, Egypt somewhere. You need to talk to the head nurse, Ms. Rachel. She will give you the real scoop on what's up . . . up there at the health center."

I close the door and walk by him and go up the stairs without saying a word. He ain't getting off that easy. I know my brother. He's thinking he can talk past his earlier indiscretion. Not this time. But he's right, I do need another opinion on Dr. Aims and the happenings at the center. I need to hear what staff thinks about both the late Dr. Aims and Ms. Flowers.

Upstairs in my bedroom, I drop to my bed and nestle my face into a pillow with the intent of calling it a night when a very pleasant thought enters my mind. I have a date with my ex-wife.

Chapter Nine

Standing at Regina's front door the reality of the situation comes down around me. Ricky was right. I have been here before. I have imagined attraction that wasn't there. Induced myself into thinking that she wanted me in a sexual manner; made myself believe that me, her, and my son being a family was something she wanted as much as I did. I was wrong, embarrassingly wrong, heartbrokenly wrong.

But she did call me sweetie, and she did say she would be flattered if I was macking her. I push her lighted doorbell and hear the soft chimes. I wait almost a minute and push it again.

I stand at the top of the mountain of stairs I had to climb to get to Regina's door. I watch a young white couple walking up Clark Street. I wonder if they live downtown, and if so . . . what type of job do they have that allows them to pay the high mortgage associated with these tall Georgians. I push the bell again, and the door is snatched open, but it's not Regina. It's her always-angry mother behind the mesh screen.

"You are going to wake up Chester ringing that bell like that. Give a person a minute to get to the door. Regina's not here, she was called out. Contact her on her mobile phone. Goodbye."

She closes the door without any further explanation.

Shrew. There is no other word for her. The woman has never treated me civil a day in her life. A class-conscious, color-struck antique who still uses a paper bag to judge a person's merit. And being darker than a paper bag myself, she excludes me from her civil and pleasant responses.

While going down the slew of front steps, I reach into my inside leather jacket pocket for my phone.

"Hey, sweetie, are you at my home?"

"Yep, just saw Mommy Dearest."

"Boy, you need to leave my mother alone. She's been nothing but good to you."

"Not in this life. Where are you?"

"I'm at the Barclay Hotel about to do an interview."

"One related to the murders?"

"Yes, I believe so, a former personal assistant to a director of a clinic."

I start to ask what clinic, but I already know what clinic and what director. Regina is on the same trail I am.

"You mind if I swing by? I wouldn't mind talking to the assistant myself."

"Oh really? You want access to one of my sources?"

I could hear her grinning over the phone.

"Didn't you pump Carol for information this morning?" I ask.

"I wouldn't say pumped."

Now there is probably an innocent child-like look on her face.

"But, you called my office and got information, right?"

I am certain her green slash gray eyes have rolled upward and away.

"Ok, ok, you're right. I do owe you. She goes on break in ten minutes. Be here and you can talk to her."

"See you in five."

*

The hotel restaurant is closed, but that is where the desk clerk directs me. I walk into a dimly lit room with small round tables covered in white linen. Regina and a young lady are seated at the third table from the door. My ex-wife beckons me over with her right index

70

finger.

The young lady has the same slant to her eyes as my business partner, Carol, but her complexion is as light as Regina's. If not for the short twist in her hair, I would have thought she was Asian or Mexican.

"Onita, this is David, my husband. I told you he would be joining us."

Not since months before the divorce has she introduced me as her husband. There is a sly smile on her face. Regina knows she has put a pause in my step with the introduction. I extend my hand to Onita which she shakes as I take a seat at the table.

"You were saying," Regina prompts Onita to continue.

"Yeah, she tried to act like she didn't have a thing for him, but everybody knew they were kicking it. She loved his dirty draws. They used to come here at least four times a month. That's how I got this job. The reservations clerk was familiar with me making Ms. Flower's reservations. She used to tell me the rooms were for friends coming from out of town. I don't even know why she bothered with such a stupid lie. But that's how she is. She thinks everybody is dumb but her.

"Dr. Aims' wife even knew about their affair, but that little crack-head didn't care, not as long as the good doctor kept bringing that money home. And his bringing home the money was due to Ms. Flowers keeping him working. She kept him working and around young Black women, and that's why he messed with her.

"He didn't love her. If it wasn't for her, he wouldn't have been around those young sisters. He used her through and through. What he wanted was a young Black girl that was down and out; they were his victims. Women he thought no one would miss."

I got questions, but it is obvious she is on a roll. So I listen.

"At first, I thought it was all about cheap sex with him. That was until the girls started coming up dead. Then I knew his ass was into something sicker. So I called the police."

"Who did you talk to?" Regina asked.

"At first, when I was working for the clinic on the Westside they sent some old white detective. But last week a Detective Lee came to see me. Back then, nobody wanted to hear what I was talking about, but now people are starting to see the truth."

"Why do you think that?" Regina asks.

"'Cause I could tell Detective Lee was serious. He asked the right question. He was hooking up the Southside murders with the Westside murders by going through the doctor's patient list. Every murdered girl found with a black ribbon around her neck had been a client of the clinic and a patient of Dr. Aims. When he saw that, Detective Lee got pissed off."

"And you said he came to see you last week?" Regina asks.

"No . . . now that I am thinking about it, it was before payday and that was two weeks ago."

I saw Regina tighten her thin lips into a frown.

"Ms. Goody-two-shoes Flowers fired me for seeing what Detective Lee saw. In my bones, I knew that doctor wasn't right. Why would a good looking white man with a wife and a director for his chick-on-the-side want to mess with crack-heads and dope fiends? It didn't make sense . . . until the girls started turning up dead. His ass was a serial killer. I will go to my grave believing that.

"And I'ma tell you this too, Ms. Flowers knew it. I laid it out for her as clear as day and she wasn't shocked. She didn't even say I was wrong, just fired me. She was so in love with his ass that she moved the truth out of her sight. But I bectha this, don't no more girls come up dead. Since he's dead, the murders are going to stop. Watch what I say."

Her beeper goes off and she stands from the table, "I got to go, y'all. Ms. Price, you know how to reach me if you need me. Nice meeting you," she says nodding her twist to me.

She stands and the bright orange of her jacket causes me to remember we are in a hotel and not just a restaurant. She walks away from the table and through the field of white linen and exits between the double swinging doors on the far side of the restaurant.

A brother like me enjoys interviews where I don't have to ask one question and still get a lot of pertinent answers.

"Well," Regina says looking at the swinging doors.

"Well indeed," I answer.

She raises her arms towards the hanging lights of the restaurant and stretches. She exhales a warm minty breath and says, "I think I need to talk to Johnny. It appears he knows more than he and Dixon have led me to believe."

Her hands go back to her lap and she brings up an ink pen sized digital recorder and cuts it off.

"Maybe Lee and Dixon were trying to keep you out of harm's way," I say smiling at the recorder and being glad I didn't ask any questions.

"No, they were covering up incompetence. If Onita saw the connection, surely a trained detective should have seen it."

She has a point.

"So you're going with Dr. Aims as the killer?"

Shaking her slender head no, she says, "Not yet. I have another source to meet with tonight. Some of what Onita said needs corroboration. There is another former employee from the Westside clinic that I need to speak with."

She lifts her purse from the floor, opens it, and drops the recording pen inside.

"I think most of what Onita said needs checking out. She was a little iffy in some areas. I find it hard to believe that Ms. Flowers would go along with the doctor being a murderer just because they were having an affair."

She looks up from closing her purse to me and says, "Matters of the heart produce strange actions, David, you know that."

If I didn't know it, her look is probing enough to inspire me to find out.

"True, but it is obvious that Onita had a little crush on the doctor too. There was some jealousy and envy in her voice for Ms. Flowers and the doctor's wife."

"I agree, and add to that a taint of vengeance. She's looking to get even with Ms. Flowers for firing her. That much is apparent, but like all sources, her statements need corroboration. I need to get moving to meet the next source."

She pushes back from the round, linen-covered table.

I'm guessing our date is off, but to check I ask, "Need a lift?"

"No, I'm meeting the source out west and after the interview I will be going to Lincoln Park and waking up Detective Lee for some truthful answers."

Yep, the date is off.

"Busy as a beaver," I say.

I am a little disappointed about the cancellation but not totally bummed. Looking into my ex-wife's face, I see both of my sons, Eric, the one that died, and Chester, the one she kept secret for almost three years. I don't know if I could have casual sex with her. My body wants her, my heart needs her, but my mind won't wrap around the act. Our past makes us deeper than casual sex. I believe my needs, in their entirety, would scare her.

I want a woman who wants a family. Regina wants a career and success. She wants a family in addition to her career. Her goal is to be the city's best reporter, then maybe a wife. I understand her ambitions, but being honest with myself . . . I realize that we have different goals.

"Yes, I am busy. Things sort of unexpectedly grew into a frenzy. But I am hoping for a rain check to discuss your real estate choices."

She gives me another probing look and smile. My ex-wife is merely flirting, nothing more.

"Are you now?" I say, being unable to restrain my own grin.

"Yes, I am," she stands up and I resist the temptation to hug her.

"Consider yourself rain-checked," I say, standing up with her, but remaining on my side of the small table.

Chapter Ten

In the morning, when I pull in front of Ricky's house, I see him in my rearview mirror. He is walking up the block at a nice pace, wearing a gold sweat suit and black running shoes. When he gets to me, he is sweating and breathing hard. My fat friend has been exercising.

When he gets to my car window, he invites me in the house, but it is such a crisp and sunny morning that I decide to sit out on his porch while he gets ready. Sweater weather, is what my grandmother called mornings like this, cool but not cold enough for a heavy jacket.

Last winter I was in Dallas on business, and I bought this blue single breasted suit from Dillard's. It was on sale, but even on sale it cost more than I was willing to pay. But I wanted it so I paid the ridiculous price, and sitting on Ricky's porch in this fall sweater weather, I am happy with the purchase.

I dressed up today to knock some of the frustration and anger out of my mind. A feeling of powerlessness got ahold of me this morning. It came with the realization that I couldn't do anything to change Babygirl being murdered and dumped behind my house, nor could I do a thing about my brother getting high, or Regina preferring Detective Lee's company over mine.

Thinking about all three happenings first thing in the morning put a brother in a deep way down in the bottom of the sewer funk. Two bowls of oatmeal with honey, butter, and raisins didn't pull me up. A hundred and fifty non-stop pushups and sit ups didn't raise me up. Five sets of fifteen rep squats with two hundred and twenty five pounds across my back, and I was still deep in the sewer.

It wasn't until I went to my closet and eyed the new blue suit that a bit of sunlight slipped into the cavernous sewer. A bit more light reached me when I noticed the black eel skin loafers that I bought in Italy last winter and still hadn't worn. I had been saving both items for a special day. I decided the day had arrived and pulled them both from my closet. So right now, a brother is as sharp as a tack and feeling damn good about it.

Ricky lives across the street from the South Shore Country Club. His home gets lake breezes and plenty of sun. I am sitting at the top of his stairs chilling in the climate when my phone rings. It is Carol.

"Good morning, partner."

"Hey, D, are you coming in this morning?"

"Shortly. I need to stop by the clinic first. What's up?"

"I don't want you to be too worried, but I had some strange dreams last night: one about you being blind, and another about a kid shooting you."

"Did you eat some pork before you went to sleep? You know that swine makes people dream."

"I don't eat pork, you know that. And by now you should take my dreams serious."

Her dreams have proved to be warnings for me in the past.

"I do take your dreams serious. It's just one has me blind, and the other has me shot. So a brother was trying to add a little levity to all the doom."

"And there was one more dream."

"Do I want to hear it?"

"A black snake took Regina. She was beating the bushes for the white one, but the black one got her."

"I'll call her now."

"Then call me back, and D, don't forget. I need to know if she is alright."

I call Regina's cell and let it ring ten times with no answer. I call her job, and her secretary tells me that she has been trying to reach her for over an hour.

When I call her home her mother says, "I thought she was with you. She didn't come home last night so I am taking Chester home with me. She can pick him up from Glenco. The both of you need to get your priorities together."

Without a goodbye, she clicks the phone off.

Then I remember Regina was going to Lincoln Park to see Detective Lee. I pull his card from my wallet and look at his number. What am I supposed to say? Hey man is my ex-wife still over there getting her freak on?

Shit. I push the buttons.

"Hello, Detective, David Price here. Is Regina with you?"

"Nope, I haven't seen her since yesterday afternoon. Why?"

"She didn't make it home last night, or to work this morning. When I left her last night she was headed out west to speak with a source."

"And you let her go alone?"

"Regina is a grown woman, and a reporter. She can handle herself."

"Obviously not if she's missing."

He too clicks off without a goodbye.

"Damn it," I stand from the steps, "Smart mouth bastard. I hope he chokes to death on his own spit. Where the hell is Regina?"

I need direction. Both Regina's investigation and mine point to the clinic and Ms. Flowers.

When Ricky comes out of his house I tell him about Regina's

situation, and he provides instant direction. He suggests that I call Regina's secretary back because Regina would have logged in where she was going last night in a book or note pad or something. I make the call and he proves correct. We get the address of 645 N. Mayfield.

*

I have the BMW humming on the Eisenhower expressway. We make it to the Austin exit from Ricky's South Shore address in less than twenty minutes. I didn't cut on the radio, and the only audible was an occasional, "Whoa," from Ricky.

When I pull in front of the address, Ricky, a solid agnostic says, "Thank you, Jesus."

I am parked behind what looks like Detective Lee's unmarked Ford. Across the street under the autumn leaved maple trees, I see Regina's new sea green Honda Accord. Coming down the steps of the two flat building, in a Wal-mart business suit, is Detective Dixon.

I hear him calling an ambulance from his cell phone. I get out the car leaving a struggling-to-exit Ricky behind.

I climb the steps passing Dixon and his protest of me entering a crime scene. I go in the same door I saw him walk out of. Inside the apartment I see Regina bound to a chair amidst huge bundles of newspapers. Her face is badly bruised, and she is not responding to Lee's words. I go straight to her and place my fingers on her neck for a pulse. There is one.

Lee drops down and begins to unbind her legs. I thumb her eyes open attempting to wake her. She is nonresponsive. There are bruises on her neck, and she has a black eye and both her cheeks are purple. I untape her hands from behind; Regina's thin wrists were bound with duct tape. Lee has freed her feet of the duct tape, and as I bend to pick

80

her up the paramedics enter.

"Don't move her," they instruct.

And I don't. I step away allowing them to do their job.

She remains unconscious as they place her on a stretcher and carry her out to the ambulance.

Ricky is standing at the door of the ambulance. I stand next to him as they load her in.

"Where are you taking her?" I ask.

"Loretto Hospital on Central Avenue," the portly paramedic next to me answers.

I open my phone and scroll down to her mother's number.

"Yes," her mother answers.

"This is David. We have found Regina unconscious. They are taking her to Loretto Hospital on Central Avenue. Can you come to her?"

"I am on my way. Thank you for calling, David. Goodbye."

I hope she doesn't bring my son to the hospital. No, she won't. More than likely she will leave him with her housekeeper.

I have learned that me being at the hospital does nothing for an unconscious patient. I can call and find out just as much as if I were there pacing a waiting room. I found Regina, and she is on her way to be treated. Now it is time for me to do my job, and find the bastard that did this to her, and that trail leads to the clinic.

*

At the clinic, Ms. Flowers has had us in the sitting area waiting for over ten minutes. Irritated, I stand and tell Ricky, "I'm going in the back to talk to a nurse. I'll be back. I get the feeling Ms. Flowers is stalling us."

He nods his big head agreeing with me, "What's going on wid de

81

nurse?" He asks while looking toward the hallway where the young man with the guns emerged yesterday.

The area has been yellow-taped off, and a uniformed officer is posted in front of the corridor.

"Robert thinks I should talk to her. He said she's the most truthful person here and will give me the real lowdown on the clinic."

I watch as Ricky surveys the busyness of the clinic. People are coming and going, but all give the yellow tape and the police officer an extended look.

"It's kind of freaky dat dey up and runnin' dis place like da doctor didn't just get his brains blown out yesterday."

I don't comment because my mind has drifted to the kid with the pistols. I need to find out who his girlfriend was or is. The kid said she overdosed on pills given to her by the doctor. If the girl died from the overdose then she too is a victim. If she is alive then she could be a source of information. I need to talk to her and Nikki.

Talking to the both of them will give me a better view of Dr. Aims, the trick. I need to see past the physician Ms. Flowers spoke of to the man who traded sex for prescriptions. Then maybe Dr. Aims, the murderer, can be seen.

And if Dr. Aims was a serial killer, how did Nikki and the kid's girlfriend survive the black ribbon? Why did he just trick off with them and not kill them in the same ritualistic fashion as the others? It's becoming clear that the more I find out about Dr. Aims, the closer I will get to who attacked Regina, and the identity of Babygirl's killer.

Regina's marks indicate that she was beaten for information. Someone tied her to a chair, questioned her, and slapped her around until they were satisfied with her answers, or until she passed out, and for that to have happened she must have been getting close to something.

All I was able to get from her secretary was the Westside address, but Detective Lee being at the two flat before us tells me he must have more information than the address. He knows whose address it is. He and his partner are either further along the same trail, or they are on a different road than the one Regina and I are traveling. I think they are further along the same trail, and they are looking back at us catching up.

I walk to the corridor with the 'Examination Room' and 'Nurses Station' signs hanging from its door jamb. Clients are sitting in the corridor in chairs that are lined against the walls. I walk to the counter of the cornered off area marked, 'Nurses Station,' by another hanging sign. Three women in maroon surgical scrubs and one woman in light blue surgical scrubs are busy behind the counter.

The one in the light blue scrubs has a name tag that reads R. Stewart, RN. The other women's name tags have full first names with no letters behind them. I am guessing that the slender lady with the slightly arched back and long silver hair is Ms. Rachel. When I get to the counter I say, "Ms. Rachel, do you have a minute?"

She looks up and over her gold wire frame half glasses from a chart and answers, "Why, Mr. David Price, for you, sir, of course I have a minute."

She walks to the counter smiling.

"Epsilon Security Service. Now that was a monthly check I was proud to write. You don't know me, but my mother was one of your first clients, her and her friends out in Harvey. That's where you started up your protection business, right?"

"Yes, Ma'am."

"My mama bragged on you every time your face popped up on the news. Whether you were behind a celebrity or a politician, it was like she had stock in your company. 'We started that boy in business,' she would say, 'He drove us old folks to the currency exchange, the bank, the grocery store, or wherever we had to go on the first of the month. Now look at him, protecting celebrities. See, a person does right and the Lord will bless him. That boy did right by protecting us old folks from them young hooligans, and now he is in the favor of the Lord.'

"Mr. Price, you could do no wrong in her eyes. She died two years ago, and she used your service up until the end, so what can I do for you today, Mr. Price? I feel like we're family."

Wow. It is usually Ricky who is recognized by people, it seldom happens to me. I must admit it feels good.

I give her a big smile and say, "Well, Ms. Rachel, I guess we are family, and you are not without a helping reputation yourself. My brother, Robert, tells me about all that you do here."

She takes a step back from the counter and looks up at me intently, "Robert? Robert Price is your brother? Well, I'll be a monkey's uncle. This is a big city but still a small town! We can't get away from each other if we tried. Lord have mercy, I knew he came from righteous stock." She steps back to the counter and places her hand atop mine, "He's a good man with a bad problem like so many others. Robert is your brother. Ain't that something? Here let me come from around here and we can go into my office and talk."

*

As soon as we walk into the tight office, I spot a familiar face in an ivory picture frame on the bookcase.

84

"Ophelia Green! That's who your mother was."

She beams a smile while nodding her head in the affirmative.

"You're right."

Ms. Rachel must be in her late sixties or early seventies herself. When I started the protection service her mama, Ms. Green, was eighty-five, so she must have lived past ninety. At eighty-five her mind was clear as a bell.

What Ms. Rachel is using as an office wasn't designed to be more than a storage room. Her bookcase takes up the majority of the west wall.

"Mama would have been tickled that you remembered her."

Ms. Rachel's slight build seems to be the appropriate fit for the closet size office. She maneuvers stealthily past me into her high-back chair behind the desk without a bump or nudge.

Sitting she says, "Now, can I assume you are here to ask me about your brother? All I can tell you is that medically things are good, for his treatment progress you will have to talk to Ms. Flowers."

She extends her hand to the brown vinyl folding chair in front of her desk. I sit with my arms dangling.

"Well, my brother isn't who I want to talk to you about. I am more interested Dr. Aims and Ms. Flowers and how they run the center."

Her eyebrows rise, and the nostrils on her pointy nose flare.

"Kind of direct, huh? No beating around the bush with you, I see. Okay, they run it as if it is a ran-for-profit business, and if they didn't run it that way, it wouldn't be open. It took me awhile to understand that.

"The leaders of our country, Mr. Price, are not overly concerned with community health. Let me tell about the miracle of what we do

85

here with the limited federal funds we receive. We run an off campus twenty-one day inpatient treatment program for both men and women. We have a shelter for the children under fifteen, so that they may be with mothers who are in the treatment facility. In that shelter, the children are fed three good meals a day and taken to school if school is in. If not we have a year-round academic tutoring program."

This tight office and armless chair are both bugging the fuck out of me. I hear what she's saying but it is hard to concentrate. The chair is so close to the desk that I can't bring up my leg. I am sitting with my hands in my lap like a kindergartner.

"After the twenty-one day inpatient program, the clients are moved to a six week outpatient program which is housed here. That is the phase your brother is currently in, and after the six weeks they go to our job development phase. Which I hear is really successful, based on what the clients tell me. They report that the jobs are not six-figure jobs, but they are steady jobs."

She rocks back in her chair hitting the wall behind her. By the indention in the dry wall, I can tell this is a constant knock.

"Now that's just drug rehabilitation services," she puts her hand out in front of her, and begins counting off fingers: "We also do early child care, offer day care service for seniors and children, pre-natal care, HIV/STD training and awareness, along with general family medicine." She closes her hand on the baby finger.

"All of this and much more is due to Ms. Flowers' creative ingenuity and grant writing skills. We draw private sector funds that support whole programs. One pharmaceutical company has agreed to fund the children's shelter for the next five years. That allowed us to get qualified teachers which opened the door for more government grants. Ms.

Flowers understands how the game is played, and she is keeping us afloat when centers across the country are drowning."

She takes a breath and webs her fingers together. She looks over my head and then back to my eyes and says, "As for Dr. Aims . . . I think his heart was in the right place, but I can't speak about other parts of his anatomy."

She gives me a smile that shows her silver capped incisor.

"As a physician he cared about people. Sixteen-hour days were not uncommon for him, but all his time spent at the clinic was not due to his Hippocratic Oath as I am sure you have heard.

"To his support, he was hired for the drug rehab program, but the man worked the whole clinic; pre-natal, family practice, HIV/STD consults, and senior consults. He worked wherever he was needed. And in addition to him being a practicing physician, he continued to do research for the pharmaceutical company that funded the children's shelter. In fact, his research was a reason the company funded the shelter. With Dr. Aims, I think Ms. Flowers took the bitter with the sweet.

"She heard the rumors like the rest of us, but he was the physician who would work in our community, and a physician who brought private sector funds. I believe she looked the other way until she couldn't.

"The murders shook us all up. She probably dismissed them on the Westside as coincidence, but when they started happening out here she had to open her eyes a little wider."

I lean forward in the folding chair and place my hands on her desk and ask, "Do you think Dr. Aims was the killer?"

Her eyelids close for a moment. When she opens them, she says, "I would hope not, but something shady was going on between him and that boy that shot him."

I sit back, "The kid said Dr. Aims had given his girlfriend drugs and she overdosed."

She gives a dismissive wave, "I wouldn't put too much stock into that. That boy had been coming around here for awhile usually at night. If he came in the daytime, Dr. Aims would hurry up and get him out of here. He didn't have a girlfriend that was a client up here, at least not one that I knew about.

"I told the police about him, but they already had him on their list. They told me he used to work at the Westside clinic as a lab technician."

The kid didn't look or sound educated at all. He played the part of a deranged, grief stricken, avenging killer rather convincingly.

"Did Ms. Flowers know him?"

"Yes, I would think she had to have seen him with them all working on the Westside together and with him coming up here so late. Late night, it was only Dr. Aims, her, and myself here tying up the day's work."

"And you are certain there was no girlfriend?"

"Not to my knowledge. That boy's business was always with Dr. Aims."

Chapter Eleven

The orange and blue plastic chairs of the waiting area are now filled, fewer clients are up and walking around, and the clock on the wall behind the security guard reads eleven o'clock. I see Ricky's finger-waved head swinging back and forth in sleep.

Looking at the guard, I wonder how it was for him coming to work this morning knowing the guy he is replacing got murdered in the same seat. I have to commend the clinic's maintenance staff. The only sign of the previous guard's demise is the spot of fresh plaster on the wall under the clock.

I need to call the hospital and check on Regina.

"Mr. Price?" a little bitty, almost midget woman has walked up to me.

"Yes."

"Ms. Flowers will see you and Mr. Brown now."

I start to send her over to wake up Ricky, but her size and child-like voice with her grown woman face might startle him into saying something hurtful.

"Thanks, dear, through that corridor?" I point to the hallway that is to the left of the one that is not yellow-taped off.

"Yes, and come all the way to the end."

The almost-a-midget lady turns and walks toward the hallway she has directed me to.

When I get to Ricky, I see that he has slobbered all down his chin onto his off white silk shirt. Everything stains silk, even spit. I shake him, and he immediately wakes up.

"We on?" he asks.

"Yep, she is in her office waiting for us."

He wipes his chin clean and stands.

"Well, don't wait fo' me. Get movin', boy."

Ms. Flower's office is four times the size of Ms. Rachel's which doesn't make it large. She is sitting behind a neat desk in a dark pink almost maroon business suit. I can see that fatigue is still claiming her face putting bags under her pretty brown eyes. Despite the festive colored suit, one can clearly see she is tired.

Ricky and I sit in two of the three chairs in front of her desk. These chairs have arms. There is only one file on her mahogany desk.

"As you requested," she pushes the file across the desk top, "the contact information for Dr. Aims' wife. I have all the drug rehabilitation clients seen by Dr. Aims listed for you as well."

Picking up the file I say, "You gave a similar list to Detective Lee, right?"

"Yes, a week ago."

"Before Dr. Aims' death, it appears Lee was already investigating the murders. So you knew the Westside deaths and the Southside deaths were more than coincidence?"

I am challenging her because I hate being played with, and she played with me last night on my porch.

"That was the police's opinion, not mine." She answers without looking at me. "If you will excuse me, I have a health center to run." She swings her chair to the computer station to her right.

She is dismissing us. The pretty Ms. Flowers is being abrupt.

"Just one more question," I say quickly, "Dr. Aims' research, what did it involve?"

Anything bringing in enough money to fund a program must be

important, and following the money always yields answers.

She turns from the station to us, "From my limited understanding, he believed addiction could be treated pharmaceutically if the patients desire to quit using drugs was sincere."

It sounds like she is saying the doctor was working on a cure for addiction.

"Wait, are you saying he was working on a cure that could control addiction?"

"No, that's not what I am saying at all. What I am saying is that my understanding of his research is limited. He did that work on his own."

"Could you provide the name of the company he was working with and a contact?"

"Victory Pharmaceuticals and a Dr. Jerome Benson." Again without looking at me, she pulls open her desk drawer and produces a card, "Here is his contact information. Good day, Mr. Price." She spins the card on the desktop.

I want to comment on her rudeness, but my mind is on the doctor's research. The cure for addiction has to be worth billions. Why do that type of work in the 'hood? I need to talk to the people at Victory Pharmaceuticals. I pick up the card from her desk and we leave her office.

*

After being dismissed, we walk outside to my car. Standing at the car, I listen to Ricky saying, "We might be goin' about dis wrong, spendin' time chasin' da kid, and da Dr.'s work buddies, and his wife. When we should be trackin' down where Babygirl was stayin' last. Ole Jumpy said da doctor had her. He had to have her somewhere."

"What good would the place he held her do?"

"If he had Babygirl dere, he might have other girls dere, or it might be somethin' dere dat could tell us what we dealin' wid here. If we find out dat da doctor did it, case closed. Somethin' at da place might nail da doctor to da cross. I'm startin' to think he was da killer. Everythang is pointin' to him."

"Could be, but you are forgetting that somebody killed him."

"All I want to know is who killed Babygirl. Da police can handle who killed da doctor."

While Ricky is talking, I see the young girl that was over Ole Jumpy's place pacing in front of the center's doors. Nikki, Robert's problem girlfriend, is sitting on a ledge talking to her. It looks like Nikki is trying to talk her into the center. I walk towards them because it is time that Nikki and I have a talk.

She is not good for my brother, and yesterday proved that. He found her, and then he got high. While she was off getting high, he was staying clean. I think his chances of staying clean are better without her, and I want her to know that that's what I think.

Steps away I hear the other girl, "No!" she yells, "All I need to do is get a couple of them pills and a little of that syrup. That stuff works, Nikki. I thought them girls was lying, but it works. I still got money. You hear what I'm telling you? I got money in my pocket, and didn't get high.

"I been clean for five days! And two days with money, I got thousands in the bank, and hundreds in my pocket, and I ain't thought about getting high until today. That stuff works, but it ain't no more at the house. I got to get out west to his wife. "

Nikki stands from the ledge and places her hands on the girl's shoulder, "It don't make sense Billie. If the pills worked why didn't he bring them up here for everybody to take?"

The girl shrugs Nikki's hands off of her shoulder and answers, "Bitch I don't know. I just need that ho's address on the Westside. The dude that was at the house said the doc got her ass clean, so she must have a stash. I only took one dose, and right now I am starting to think about getting high, so it must be wearing off."

"You know two of the girls that went to stay at the house is dead now?"

"Fuck them. I was dead snorting that shit. For five days I been alive, and doing real shit."

"Maybe if you go inside and tell Ms. Flowers about the pills and stuff she might know what to do."

"Ms. Flowers trying to get a bitch in group, I been through all that. That shit Dr. Aims made is the lick, it's a cure fo' real."

"But the other girls that took it is dead!"

"His wife ain't. You ain't hearing me, Nikki. I took one dose, and I ain't tooted no dope, or smoked a crack-rock in five days. It worked, just like Doc said it would. I will take a pill and a table spoon full of syrup over crack-rocks and heroin any day."

"And you feel okay?"

"Like new money. I ain't even dope sick, but I feel it coming. That's why I got to get out west. The Doc's wife is still alive. She the only one who might know how to get some, with him being dead. I ain't going backwards Nikki . . . I'm moving. . . . "

The girl stumbles and falls over.

Nikki tries to catch her, but the girl hits the sidewalk like biscuit dough.

When I get to her, she is stretched out and limp. I check for her pulse, and it's barely there. I slap her, no response. I shake her but still nothing.

Nikki yells, "Billie!" but the girl is deaf to her. I thumb open her eyes and they are just as blank as Regina's were. I don't think we have time to wait for an ambulance. I scoop her up and am carrying her to my car.

I yell to Ricky, "Get us to a hospital!"

*

Ricky is behind the wheel and I am in the back with the girl, and Nikki is in the front seat with him. We are on Ashland Avenue, and he must have the BMW floored because we are flying. The girl hasn't mumbled a sound, and her breathing is shallow. When we get to 95th Street, Ricky makes a right. He must be going to Little Company of Mary.

Screaming tires are heard behind us. Looking out the window, I see a white van moving just as fast as we are. It doesn't slow down, and now it is gaining.

"Ricky!"

"I see it, man! He's been on our tail since the center."

Ahead, traffic is stopped at the light on Damen. The van doesn't slow down.

"He's going to ram us!" I yell.

Parked cars to the right and traffic to the left, we are sitting ducks. I pull the girl to me and brace for the crash. The van slams into the back of us, forcing our car into the bus in front of us. The bus pulls onto the sidewalk, but the van continues to drive us into the intersection.

"Motherfucker!" Ricky yells.

94

Ricky and Nikki's seat belts hold them in place. The back window has shattered. I can see the driver of the van. It's the kid that shot the doctor. He has shoved us into oncoming traffic. Ricky is trying to pull away, but the van is locked to us. The kid bails out from behind the van's driver's seat.

It's a damn semi-trailer heading towards us. Ricky opts for the parked cars; we barrel through them and he steers through the plate glass window of a dry cleaners. We crash into the store's back wall. Air bags fire from all around us. I am still holding the girl when I hear gunfire from behind. Bullets are puncturing the air bags.

"Motherfucker, do you know, . . ." now I hear shots from the front of the car, "who you fuckin' wid?"

"Uhg!"

More shots from the front, then I hear the thud of a body falling.

"Dumb ass motherfucka!"

More shots.

The passenger door is yanked open, and I see Nikki stabbing the air bags with a box cutter. She assists me in getting the girl out of the back of the car.

There is blood, but not from gunshots. The girl and I have cuts. We get her out of the car and onto the carpeted floor of the cleaners. I walk around my totaled BMW to the driver's side and find Ricky sitting against the hanging fender. He is bleeding from his gut and left shoulder. The kid is laid on his back with his chest open and the top of his face smashed in. I go to Ricky.

"Can you stand?"

"Hell naw, da nappy-headed bastard shot me three times, twice in my gut, and once in the shoulder. But I betcha his short-dick ass won't get off another round. I betcha dat."

Then he slumps over.

"Ricky!"

He extends his feet out, stretching his legs straight, and he says "Nigga, I ain't dead. I'm aw'ight. Don't start dat yellin' shit!"

Chapter Twelve

No, he ain't dead, but he is far from alright. Him being obese saved his life and added complications. The doctors removed all three bullets, and said his girth stopped the bullets from passing through internal organs and causing more damage.

However, while he was in recovery a blood clot moved, and he suffered a massive heart attack. He had to have another operation to remove the clot. They put a stent in a chest artery, and in his groin area.

The doctor has been trying to convince Ricky's wife, Martha, to persuade him to have the gastric bypass surgery once he recovers from the gunshot wounds and heart attack. But I will bet a hundred dollar bill to a doughnut that once Ricky is released, nobody will get him close to a hospital anytime soon.

The girl, Billie, is going to be okay. It seems she has been to Little Company of Mary before. The doctor immediately ordered blood work looking for opiates, suspecting that she had overdosed. What they found were toxic levels of naturally occurring opiates in her blood.

Somehow her brain had released natural opiates to a toxic level. The doctor injected her with a dopamine inhibiter and that brought her around. I asked the doctor could she share the information with Regina's doctor at Laretto Hospital, and she didn't hesitate to make the call. The last report had Regina's pulse, and blood pressure rising.

The kid that shot the doctor and forced us into traffic is dead, and I know I should feel some sympathy, or least empathy for the young Black brother, but I feel nothing of the kind. He tried to kill Ricky, the girl, Nikki, and me. I'm not glad the little fucker is dead, but my heart isn't feeling a loss.

Bowlegged Nikki and I were treated for superficial scratches and cuts. My new blue suit is ruined with too many rips and scuffs to count. We are now sitting in one of the hospital's family waiting rooms going over the car crash and the shooting with Detectives Lee and Dixon.

It is not a large waiting area, so we are all in close proximity to each other. I am close enough to smell Lee's sandalwood body oil. Both cops are sitting relaxed on the sofa, and Nikki and I are in the floral patterned armchairs. The television that is hanging from the ceiling is playing a Sanford and Son rerun, but it is on mute. I would rather hear Red Foxx than either Dixon or Lee.

I can't figure out why, but these cops are beating around the bush, and a brother is too tired, too sore, and too frustrated to continue listening to the bull that is coming out their mouths. I need to get to Regina, and the detectives are wasting my time. Nikki and I have been recanting identical statements for the last fifteen minutes, and these officers of the law are continuing to talk in circles.

"There are more than enough witnesses willing to corroborate your stories," a black-leather-jacket-wearing Lee says.

As if witnesses are going to be a problem. A whole busload of people saw the kid force us into the intersection.

"It appears Dion Jacobs snapped once it became obvious that we were onto him as the Ribbon Killer," Lee continues.

After he says 'Ribbon Killer,' he sits erect on the sofa. He is notifying us of the importance of his labeling the kid murderer. His sitting up causes me to sit back. Being almost check to check with my ex-wife's boyfriend is not a desirable position.

Turning his red-dreadlocked head to me, he says, "That was Dion Jacobs' apartment where we found Regina. I am certain he assaulted her due to her investigation."

Nikki turns in her autumn-flowered armchair towards Detective Lee with her eyebrows crinkled and eyes squinted into a questioning expression and asks, "But why was this Ribbon Killer trying to kill Billie? She wasn't investigating anything."

A damn good question, one which I am certain Lee won't answer with any real information. I think he is keeping all the real information close to his vest.

"That's unclear at this point," he answers, "Perhaps he thought she could link him to the other murders? And we can't assume Billie was his target."

To me he says, "He may have been after Mr. Price and Mr. Brown. You guys were investigating the murders after all. You probably got close enough to be a threat."

That's bullshit. That kid was after Billie. Ricky and I just happened to be there and got in his way. He followed us from the health center after we had Billie in the car. I'm certain she was the target, not us.

Attempting to get some info on the good doctor, I ask, "So Jacobs and Dr. Aims were working together? What, they were some kind of killing team that turned on each other?"

Dixon sits up from his relaxed position on the sofa and says, "No. We believe Jacobs killed Dr. Aims because he was beginning to suspect him as the murderer."

"What?" is my knee-jerk response. He is pointing me to China, far away from the doctor, and solely to Jacobs.

Dixon continues with, "Yes, um, we believe Dr. Aims was doing a preliminary investigation of his own, and that's what brought on Jacobs' actions. Jacobs went after the doctor the same way he attacked

Regina and your group. Dr. Aims was a victim. Jacobs acted alone in these hideous crimes."

Lee will not even make eye contact with me after Dixon offers this explanation.

For the hell of it I say, "Then one can assume it's over, no more murdered Black girls with black ribbons around their necks?"

"That's right. It's over," Dixon says standing.

There it is. That's what the beating around the bush is about. These lazy clowns are trying to slam dunk the case, and wrap it up with a big bow. My agreeing that it's over is part of the big bow. The last thing a closed case needs is me or Regina snooping around it, and they think that stopping me is the first step to stopping Regina. Lee should know better. Once Regina is dug in, she's in deep and committed.

To be as much of an irritant to them as they are to me, I say, "I'm just curious, did you ever find a common cause of death among the girls?"

Dixons forehead wrinkles and his nose ripples as a grimace moves across his dark bumpy face. He has both razor bumps and acne. He is looking down at me as if I am a pile of dog shit on his white carpet. "The coroner is still looking into to that," he mumbles.

To add to his annoyance, I say, "You may want the coroner to search for toxic levels of natural opiates. That appeared to be the problem with Billie and Regina. Perhaps Jacobs injected the murdered girls with the same toxin."

I purposely don't mention Dr. Aims' research. The less they think a brother knows the better. If they want to pass the good doctor off as an innocent, so be it. Less interference from them while I dig for the truth. The doctor and his research are starting to smell foul to me, real

100

damn foul.

I am not a doctor, but I know that naturally occurring opiates in the body don't render people unconscious. Something brought the opiates to toxic levels, and that question points to the good doctor and his research.

Dixon is looking toward the door-less doorway into the hall and answers me with, "Yes, well, he was a lab technician. It is possible. We will look into it. However, we don't need anything to cloud the fact that the murders are over at this point. One more psycho is off the street."

He hikes up the pants of his cheap brown suit. "This case is closed," he states, almost bragging.

Lee stands with his partner and asks, "You guys feel up to talking to the press? We are making a statement in front of the hospital. Would you like to join us?"

They won't get me lying on camera, "No, I'll pass, but Nikki?"

"No. That's okay." Nikki answers.

Walking towards the doorway with Dixon, Lee says, "You guys are free to go. Leave whenever you want."

Once the detectives are completely out of the waiting room, bowlegged Nikki turns to me and says, "That's bullshit. I mean really. And they the police?" She looks like somebody just told her there wasn't a Santa Claus.

I lift up one of the bandages on my arm and look at the cut. I tell her, "They want it to be over, and the killings have stopped, so it's over." I press the bandage back down. I got two on my left arm, one on my right, one on the top of my baldhead, and the last one is at the base of my neck.

The paramedics had to cut Nikki's left khaki pant leg open to bandage her knee. She has a square bandage covering her chin, and a small one behind her right ear. Her white sweatshirt is blood stained down the front. My guess is the wound from her chin caused the stain. Looking at her all scratched up and bruised, I decide against telling what I think about her being around my brother. That can wait.

"But all they got is the 'who,' David, without the 'why'. What about why? Why did all those girls die?"

People don't care about the why is what I should tell her. Investigating the why would mean they are trying to prevent future crimes. Investigating the why would mean that people would see each other as human beings and equals. Investigating the why would mean city bureaucracy would be as concerned about a young poor Black girl dying as it would a young rich white girl.

No, people only want the 'who.' Finding the 'who' stops the immediate pain. The why is work, and people ain't gonna work.

"They think the 'why' is that Jacobs was a psychopathic serial killer."

Nikki shakes her head negating my statement, and causing her platted braids to swing.

"No, David, the 'why' is that stuff Dr. Aims was giving them girls. Tasha was taking that stuff and she got murdered. Lynette was taking that stuff and she got murdered. Billie was taking that stuff and she almost got murdered. That stuff is the 'why,'" she says with eyes wide and bright.

What she is calling the stuff, I am guessing is the doctor's research, and little bowlegged Nikki might be on to something.

"That's not the 'why' the police are going to tell the media. They want it over."

I flip my phone open thinking about calling out to Regina's hospital.

"Is it over for you, David?"

Is it over for me? Am I done looking for why a young Black girl, my best friend's niece, was found dead behind my house? Am I done looking for why my ex-wife was tied to a chair and beat? Am I done looking for why a kid shot my best friend? Am I done doing my part to make my community safer for my women?

How could I be? I promised Ricky's sister, Brenda, I would find out who killed her daughter. That may be done, but she too will want more than the who. She is going to want the why.

"No, Nikki . . . it ain't over for me."

Chapter Thirteen

I hear the chime of the elevator in the hall, and Ms. Flowers walks through the door-less doorway into the waiting room with my business partner, Carol.

I don't remember if I called Carol back or not. Looking down at my Rolex I see it's five fifteen. The last time I was aware of the time it was eleven o'clock in the morning. Ricky and I were at the health center waiting to talk to Ms. Flowers, and the kid murderer was only a disturbing thought.

Carol sits in the armchair next to me. She smells like spring, like lilacs.

"When I left Larreto, Regina had regained consciousness. Her mother was with her." She places her hand on mine.

"Good," I say.

"Her mother's housekeeper has agreed to stay overnight with Chester. I asked to pick him up, but she refused saying he would be more comfortable with the housekeeper. I didn't argue with her."

"Was Regina talking?"

"Yes, she identified her attacker as the person she went to interview. She said once she began listing the names of the girls that were murdered, he flipped out. He hit her so hard that she saw stars, and when she came to, she was tied to a chair.

"He questioned her about who else knew about all the girls, and the murders happening on both the Westside and Southside of the city. Then he started asking her about another girl, a girl that wasn't on her list. When she told him she knew nothing of the girl, he injected her in the shoulder through her blouse. Even in her sick bed, she was quite upset about her new chiffon blouse getting blood stained."

Ms. Flowers, who is sitting next to Nikki on the sofa, asks Carol, "Did she recall the other girl's name?"

"A Smith something," Carol replies looking at Ms. Flowers with a smile of recognition; she is expecting a greeting from her.

"Billie Smith?" Nikki asks.

"Yes, that's it, Billie Smith." Carol answers Nikki, and sits forward in the love seat raising an index finger in Ms. Flower's direction, but stops short of speaking.

I know Carol, and I can tell a thought has crossed her mind and that thought has stopped whatever comment she was going to make to Ms. Flowers. She sits back in the love seat and places her hand in her lap atop her long, navy blue skirt. Her legs are crossed at the ankles, and her black pumps look freshly polished. We take our shoes to the same shoeshine guy on 81st and Racine.

Nikki, who is wearing tattered gym shoes, looks at me again with eyes wide open and says, "And we know why he's asking about her don't we, David?"

"Huh?" I don't have a clue.

I don't get what she thinks I get. Nikki exhales heavily, smacks her lips, and shakes her head from side to side as if I am a mentally slow cousin that she has to help tie his shoe.

"She's the only one that took that stuff that is still alive . . . and she almost didn't make it."

Oh, now I get it. Remembering the conversation I heard between her and Billie outside of the center, I say, "The doctor's wife is still alive," thinking it more than speaking it.

"What stuff are you talking about, Nikki?" Ms. Flowers asks.

"Nothing," Nikki says standing from the sofa.

It didn't occur to me to ask why Ms. Flowers is here until Nikki moves away from her. To my knowledge Billie Smith isn't a client of the center.

And as if she hears my thoughts, Ms. Flowers says, "Your crash made the early evening news, Mr. Price. Ms. Rachel, my charge nurse, made me promise to come see about you after we saw the condition of your car, and heard that Mr. Brown was seriously injured.

"And once we heard your name, Nikki, we all agreed that someone from the clinic should come up here. Not that we drew straws or anything. We are all concerned, and we want to make sure that you have a ride back to the shelter this evening. This has been a very trying day for you, Nikki."

Ms. Flowers' tone is as sympathetic as a worrying grandmother, and the look on her face is Big Mama maternal. If I was Nikki, I would sit back down on the couch believing Ms. Flowers had nothing but my best interest at heart. Her whole effect is caring.

Nikki sits on the far end of the sofa however and says, "I was going to stay with David tonight. He needs me to bandage the wound on the back of his neck and help him up the stairs to his house. He was going to call and ask you was that okay."

The lie is so sudden it startles me a little, partly because I am still under Ms. Flowers' Big Mama influence. But obviously Nikki isn't influenced in the slightest.

I catch up to the situation and say, "Yes, I was about to call when you walked in."

Ms. Flowers looks to me, Carol, then to Nikki, and says, "I guess it would be okay under the circumstances, but you must be on time for the eight o'clock group in the morning."

"I will," Nikki answers.

"And Robert, too," Ms. Flowers says to me.

"They will both be there, Ms. Flowers," I add with a smile.

"Okay," she says patting her lap with palms, "I am happy to see that you both are no worse for wear. According to the police, Mr. Price, things are over. Do you agree? Did the threat end with the death of that young man?"

The way she says young man with absolutely no trace of familiarity in her tone causes the smile to leave my face. Ms. Flowers is going on like she has never met the kid. I hate being lied to. Ms. Rachel plainly stated that it would be almost impossible for Ms. Flowers not to know Jacobs, not only from the Westside clinic, but from the late nights at the Southside clinic as well. Enough is enough.

"You knew the kid, Ms. Flowers. He was in your employ at the Westside clinic. He worked in the lab. And you had to have seen him during some of late meetings he had with Dr. Aims at the Southside center."

She looks into my eyes and says, "No. You are mistaken. It wasn't the same person. You are speaking of Dion Jacobs. He was our lab technician on the Westside, and he is still very much alive."

How far is she going with this?

I tell her, "You might want to go down to the morgue and see the young man, or maybe even talk to the police."

She flips her hair from beneath her dark pink suit jacket.

"There is no need, because I know Dion. The kid who came in the clinic and shot Dr. Aims was not him. You are mistaken. Perhaps you and the police should check your facts a bit more thoroughly. Good evening, Mr. Price." She turns from me and stands.

"Well, who was the kid, and where is Dion?" I ask.

She turns back around. My direct questions haven't disturbed the calming expression on her face. She remains pleasant and consoling.

"I have no idea who the kid was, but Dion Jacobs was staying with Dr. Aims, assisting him in his research. Dr. Aims has, or rather had, a laboratory in the area. A converted home and Dion was staying there."

"Do you have the address?" Nikki and I simultaneously ask.

"No, but I am sure Dr. Aims' wife does." Clearing her throat, she steps closer to me, and sits on the corner of the love seat next to my chair.

In a quieter voice she says, "Mr. Price, I am not the bad guy here. I am not the one distorting truths in this situation. Whatever is going on is affecting the clinic and our clients. I want to get to the bottom of it as badly as you do. I hope you consider me an ally, as I do you." She pauses and again looks me in the eyes. Although she had my attention prior, having those pretty eyes focused on me draws my total concentration.

She continues with, "Some questions have arisen that do have me concerned as center director, and after I have investigated further I would appreciate your confidence. Could we meet later tonight? Either my place or yours?"

She is sincerely asking for my help. And like Ricky, I am weak for a damsel in distress, so I painfully reach around to my hip pocket and pull out my wallet and retrieve a business card for her.

"No problem," I say, "Call me when you're ready." The reaching motion has brought additional pain to my already aching shoulder and chest.

She takes the card and stands.

"I'll see you later tonight." She nods goodbye to the others in the waiting area and leaves through the door-less doorway.

If Ms. Flowers is being truthful, which I believe she is, I need to go talk to Dr. Aims' wife immediately. Either the cops are misinformed about the kid, or they are perpetrating a great miscarriage of justice.

Once Ms. Flowers is out of earshot, Carol says, "Her name is Sandra Flowers, and she graduated with me from Gage Park High School in 1992. She was a nerd, president of the math club, started a Latin translation club, and she was a debate team member.

"Sandra Flowers was the brain of our class, but the girl had no social skills. I guarantee you that she doesn't remember me even though we went to high school together for four years. Back then, her face stayed in a book or behind a computer scene. We nicknamed her Professor Frog because of her eyes and her brain."

Nikki giggles, "We call her Frog too, Boss Frog."

I see nothing frog-like about Ms. Flower's eyes, doe-like but nothing amphibian.

"David," Nikki stops giggling. "What are you going to do now?"

"Yes, D, what are you going to do?"

Chapter Fourteen

What I did was have Carol take me to a car rental service where I rented a steel grey Chrysler 300. Then I dropped Nikki off at my place with my brother. I changed into some jeans and my black White Sox windbreaker. I dropped two extra .9mm clips into my front pockets and then I drove to the hospital to check on my ex-wife. On the drive to the hospital, I couldn't help but think about Nikki.

Through the course of the day, I have developed a respect for her. She is smart and more mature than I thought. From our conversations today, I wouldn't have thought she had a drug problem. During the car ride home, she told me that she pursued my brother in their relationship. It appears that in their circle of acquaintances my brother is a "baller," a big spender, with a generous heart.

She told me, "We had a little place and everything for awhile. Then his money ran out, and we went to floating from place to place, and hustling here and there, but we stayed together after his money was gone, and that surprised me. I surprised myself by not leaving him when his money ran out, and he surprised me by wanting to still take care of me after the party was over.

"We was a couple before me or him really knew it. When he told me he loved me, the words made me cry because I believed him. We was smokers, David, serious smokers who got high every day, crack-fare came before everything, and that was a truth we both understood.

"Then one day, we was in this abandoned garage that was home for right then. Rain was falling in all around us, and the place reeked of people piss, dog piss, and rotten wood. A badly beaten Pit Bull had claimed a corner of the garage.

"I looked at where we was. I mean I really looked at it. I told Robert that we could do better than sharing a place with a dog. I told him it was time for us to do better because I wanted to have his baby. And I do. I want to have a child with him, but I don't want to have a crack-baby, or a baby the State has to take because I am all cracked out. I want to love my child, and all crack lets you love is crack.

"God gave me and Robert something special. Our thing wasn't suppose to last with both of us smoking crack like we was, but it did, and I think the best gift we can give God is a child that came from the love he let us have."

Yep, little bowlegged Nikki made me see past her being a crack-head . . . to her being my brother's woman. And for the first time in a long while . . . I envy my brother.

*

When I get to my ex-wife's hospital room, I walk in to find Detective Lee sitting in the only visitor's chair in the room.

"She's asleep," he says to me but looking at Regina, "been that way for a minute. The nurse said she will probably sleep through the night because even though she was unconscious she hasn't rested. I didn't understand that." He runs both hands through his dreadlocks bunching them up then letting them fall over his shoulders.

"Hey, Price, I don't blame you for this happening to her. I didn't mean to come off like that." He looks up to me briefly, but returns his gaze to Regina.

I don't respond because I want him to leave. I want to sit in that chair and be alone with Regina.

He unbuttons his jean jacket and slides it off and hangs it on the back of the chair.

"This case is bigger than me and my partner. We are only soldiers following orders. I told Regina that, but she wouldn't listen. I think what's going on here is bigger than the clinic and the doctor. My partner and I were told the kid's name before we even got to your wreck. We were told the case was closed with his death. We have already been reassigned."

He quickly glances his grayish green eyes up to me as if he is checking to make sure I am listening.

"Between me and you in this room, I think it stinks and my partner does too, but we are soldiers, and we follow orders. If I wasn't a soldier, say I was a concerned citizen who didn't have to follow orders, it would bother me that that kid wasn't Dion Jacobs."

He retrieves his phone from his pants pocket, and thumbs through some function. The phone seems to be something for him to look at other than me while he's talking to me.

"If I was just a concerned citizen, I would be aware of the fact that that kid worked for Dion Jacobs and the doctor. I would get Billie Smith out of the hospital before something happens to her, and I would talk to the doctor's wife who is held up at her grandfather's at 8754 South St. Lawrence.

"I would figure that the doctor's wife must be scared, and guess that she has enough money to leave the city soon. I would realize that what or who I was up against is big enough to call shots within the police department. I would proceed with extreme caution and secrecy. I would think a reporter with a cop boyfriend was safe, and my attention would be on the nosy center director, and the young Black girls that have no protection."

He powers his phone down, and doesn't look up at me.

He reaches down, and looses the laces on his white Air Force Ones, and leans back in the chair causing it to recline all the way back. It is obvious that he's not going anywhere, but he has issued me marching orders.

Before I turn to leave I say, "Have her call me when she wakes up."

"No problem. I'll be right here."

One would think that gratitude for the information he just gave me would stop me from wanting to bust his head open to the white meat, but it doesn't. The thought of him hanging around until Regina wakes up pisses me off. It's going to look like he's here for her while I am off doing my thing.

I leave without saying another word. I can't make a thank you come from my mouth, and calling him a nappy headed, high yellow, red bastard for hanging around my ex-wife wouldn't be the appropriate thing to do. I reconcile myself with knowing that Regina is a smart woman, and once all this mess is cleared up, she will recognize the truth.

*

I have been on the go for over twelve hours, and every movement is felt in aches, but a second wind is moving through me with the information from Lee. Walking through the hospital's dimly lit parking lot my mind is formulating a plan of action. The first problem is how to get Billie Smith out of the hospital and under my protection.

Looking at the clock on the 300's dashboard, it reads 8:25. By the time I get to the hospital out south it will be after 9:00, and visiting hours will be over. And who's to say that Billie Smith will believe that she's in danger and safer with me. I push the sedan over eighty miles per hour on the expressway and decide to worry about the situation once I get there.

*

I park in the E.R. parking lot, and enter through that entrance as well. I make it through the crowded corridor and to the elevator bank without being stopped. When I get on the elevator, I hear chimes over the hospital's speaker system, and a female voice states that visiting hours are over. I exit on the fourth floor hoping they haven't moved her to another room.

When I enter her room, Billie is sitting up, and she is wide awake and looking at the News at Nine. It suddenly occurs to me that she doesn't know me from Adam. She was out cold when we carried her to the car and all through the crash and the shooting. I should have had Nikki call her with an introduction.

She looks from the television to me as if she does know me, so I decide to be direct, "We got to get you out of here," I tell her.

"I know, right? Shit feels creepy for real. Where is Nikki?"

She swings her bony legs from under the sheet to the side of the bed.

"She's with Robert at my house."

"You Robert's brother, ain't you? The one that lives on Throop Street, not the one that lives out east. I was with him a couple of times when he came over to get cash from you. Me and Robert used to party some before Nikki took him over."

My brother and I have an understanding. When he is truly in need of money for drugs, he is to come see me before committing a crime. I'd rather get him high than get him out of jail.

"Yep, that's me, I'm David. And it was Nikki and I that brought you here."

115

"Yeah, I saw you and her in the E.R . . . thanks for that."

My brother's taste in women is becoming apparent, young and slim seems to be his preference. Nikki and Billie could pass for sisters, except Billie's hair is wavy and light brown. She has what Black people call good hair.

"Where are your clothes? We need to get you out of here."

"Ain't nothing left but my sweat pants. They cut my shirt open in the E.R."

She stands up from the bed and strips right out of the hospital gown and goes to the closet nude. She is definitely a member of the Itty Bitty Titty Committee. I doubt that either breast would fill a tea cup.   She hops into her grey sweat pants and slides her tiny feet into a pair of black flip flops.

I take off my Sox jacket to give to her, and her eyes immediately go to my holstered pistols. Wearing the guns is second nature to me. I often forget the effects of seeing guns on those that don't live with them. There is no way I can walk through the hospital hallways strapped. I take off my pistols and white t-shirt.

"Damn. You in good shape, David."

She doesn't hesitate to run her hands over my shoulders and down my arms and across my abs. And I can't lie, her quick caress does make a forty-one year old brother's brain pause and body shiver. She has a soft graceful touch.

"Big muscles run in y'all family, huh?" She asks with a hand lingering on my abs. "Robert ain't got the shoulders and arms, but he got nice stomach muscles like you."

I step back because her eyes tell me she isn't afraid to let her hand drop further south for more family comparison. I hand her the t-shirt

116

and slip the double holster and pistols over my bare skin.

She returns my Sox jacket to me, and pulls the t-shirt over her head and upper torso. Her nipples are protruding against the white t. She bites off the hospital wrist band and says, "Let's go."

We walk down the busy corridor and past the busier nurse's station unnoticed. She breaks into giggles when get on the elevator. "Sorry" she says, "I laugh when I'm nervous."

When I was a kid, I did too, so I understand. And she is a kid, I remind myself. She is a kid with a drug problem, and a young sister who needs my protection.

In the rental car, my cell phone vibrates, but I can't answer because I'm pulling into traffic on 95th Street. At the light, I answer and hear, "Mr. Price, someone is following me!"

"Are you sure, Ms. Flowers?"

"Yes, since I left the Westside clinic."

"Where are you now?"

"On 63rd and Ashland heading to your house. I think I should go to the police."

"No. Just stay on the line with me, and continue towards my place. How close is the car?"

"It's an SUV, and they are right behind me!"

"Can you make out who is in the vehicle?"

"All I can see is one white man."

"Turn down a southbound one-way going north, and don't signal, just make the turn."

I hear her wheels squeal.

"Did you make a turn?"

"Yes."

"Are they still behind you?"

"No."

"Good, go to my house. Robert will meet you at your car. Stay on the line while I call him."

I push in my home number and Robert answers on the fifth ring, "Go outside, man, Ms. Flowers should be pulling up. Take Yin and Yang with you. She's being followed. Get her in the house fast. I'll be there in a minute."

I click back over to Ms. Flowers.

"He's waiting for you."

"I'm two blocks away from your house. I don't see the SUV anymore."

"Good. See you in a minute."

I keep the phone to my ear just in case.

"Are you still there?" She asks.

"Yes."

"Okay, I see Robert and your dogs. I'm parking in front of your driveway."

I don't tell her not to because in the rental car I would have to open the underground door from inside the house.

"You're safe now," I say and click off.

I don't know how true that is for her, or any of us involved in this case: cops being pulled off the case, a murdered mad scientist doctor doing suspect research, a white man in an SUV following people, and dead young Black girls in the middle of it all, no one is safe.

Suspect research. That's putting it mildly. I believe Dr. Aims was experimenting with those young girls and they probably died due to his research.

What was it Billie said at the hospital . . . 'Shit feels creepy for real.'

Chapter Sixteen

I park behind the Volvo. It's time for me and the pretty Ms. Flowers to discuss the pharmaceutical company that was sponsoring the doctor's research. I need to know everything she knows.

Billie opens the car door on her side, "Hey, um, David, I need to run down the street for a minute," she says.

I have watched her fidgeting during most of the drive, and when we passed the Reeds', the dope dealer's house on my block, I saw her fist clench, and then I remembered her conversation with Nikki in front of the center.

She told Nikki that she had been drug free for five days due whatever Dr. Aims gave her, but the effects had worn off and she wanted to get high.

I guess seeing a dope house triggered her craving with increased intensity. I need to proceed with caution, and choose my words carefully because her addiction is pulling her away from me, and the safety I can provide.

I hope the look on my face shows the true concern I have for her, as she is not safe on these streets, "I am not sure leaving me is the safest thing to do right now. We have to identify the threat. It is obvious that you are a target. We just don't know who is doing the hunting. Understand?"

She has one foot out of the car, and on the curb.

"You can go with me. I'll be right out. Do you party? I got money. We can run and get a couple of bags, then come right back. And me you can find some place to be alone in your house. Trust me, David, you will have a good time."

I hear the desire in her voice, and if I didn't know better I would think the desire was for me, but the grown man that I am does know better. This young lady wants to get high despite the apparent threat. She is an addict, and from dealing with my brother I have learned that direct denial will only incite her to battle.

So I tell her, "Sounds good, but do you really think this is the right time? The SUV that was following Ms. Flowers could easily make the block, and spot you. An attempt was made on your life once today. The threat is serious. Despite the very tempting offer, I think we would be safer inside. At least for now, do you agree?"

And as if on cue, a black SUV turns onto the block.

I tell her, "get down," and draw my pistol from the right holster. She doesn't hesitate to pull her leg back into the car and hunch down.

The SUV slows while passing the Volvo, but doesn't stop. It stops at the end of the block makes a u-turn, and parks on the opposite side of the street facing my house. They are either staking out the Volvo, my house, or calling in for orders. I draw my other pistol. The light from my front door opening flashes in the corner of my eye. I look to see my brother and my dogs in the doorway.

"Go to my house and stay low," I tell Billie.

She doesn't hesitate to move out. She's up the stairs before I can make it around the rental car. I close her door, and click the key pad for the alarm. When I look to the porch she has made it to my brother. I signal him to take her in, and close the door. Holstering my pistols, I walk down the sidewalk towards the SUV.

I am not walking down the block for confrontation, but for information. Whoever is in this vehicle is part of the threat. And for me to continue the investigation, the threat must be identified. A brother needs to know who is in the ring with him.

The new neighbors that moved in next door to Fred and Bonnie are out enjoying the cool crisp night air. The neighbors are a senior couple in their late seventies, newlyweds according to Fred. I wave and they both wave back from their lawn chair rockers. That was the new thing this summer, most of the neighbors have lawn furniture on their porches.

The newlywed seniors only have two rockers, some folks however have the long reclining loungers, and little cabana tables next to them. I was thinking about getting a lounger myself until I thought about Regina's or her mother's possible comments concerning the inappropriateness of yard furniture on the front porch.

Other than the newlyweds, the people in the SUV, the one lone pedestrian making it towards the Reeds' house, and me, the block is unoccupied. I am on the opposite side of the street of the SUV. They must see me approaching because the drivers' window is being rolled down. I walk out into the street, and head for the opening window.

The red hair and redder face of Paul Phillips is seen in the peachy light of the street lamps. He's actually grinning at me.

"Hey there, David Price, I thought that was your house she parked in front of." He opens the driver's door exiting the SUV.

Flooding, that is the word. The man is flooding. His suit pants are at least two inches above his black wingtips. His checkered socks are clearly seen. Smiling and still approaching, I extend my hand.

"Long time no see, Paul."

We shake hands and I am relieved. Paul Phillips is not a threat. He is a white private detective that works both the South and Westside of the city which means his clientele his mostly Black. The SUV is a step up for him, a serious step up. Last time I saw him was in a rusted '90 Camry.

"Nice ride, man."

"Yeah, it is, aye? I got it last week, been working insurance cases lately. Damn good money. Cutting into your racket on this case though, I got hired to watch and keep safe the lady bird that ran into your house."

"Who?"

"The Flowers dame, you know her, aye?"

"Who hired you?"

"Come on, Price."

"No, you come on. Girls are dying around this case."

I am not playing the client privilege game with him, and I hope my tone reflects my seriousness.

"Victory Pharmaceuticals is the client," he answers looking down at the ground.

"They hired you to protect her?"

"Surveillance mostly, but they want to make sure she stays alive. They are expecting some bad press, and her death would add to it. Don't know too much more, got the job this morning, but it came with a tag along." He thumbs toward the SUV.

I look through the window and see the face of the kid that shot Ricky and Doctor Aims.

"He's some sort of consultant with the company. He found the dame easy enough though."

I walk past Paul to the open window of the SUV.

"Dion Jacobs?"

"Nope, Dion Jacobs is dead. He got gunned down in an altercation today."

"And you are?" I ask the kid.

"Me, you want to know who I am, Mr. Price?"

He pauses, and pulls his wallet from his hip pocket. It doesn't surprise me that the kid knows my name. I am getting the feeling that I am the least informed person involved.

"Why, I am Roger Franklyn from Oakland, California, and that's Franklyn with a 'y.'"

His whole dark, narrow face opens up with a smirk.

I step away from the SUV because I want to do something evil to the kid, something real motherfucking evil because he's playing some sort of game and people are dying. Not to mention that the little fucker probably tied Regina to a chair and beat her.

To Paul I say, "Why don't you come on in for a cold beer. That way you can keep a better eye on your subject. We wouldn't want her to slip out the back on you, and bring your tag-along too."

"Aye?"

"Yeah, come on in. She knows you are following her anyway."

I want Ms. Flowers, and Dion Jacobs aka Roger Franklyn in the same room when I start asking the hard questions.

Chapter Seventeen

Everybody is in the front room when we enter: my brother, Nikki, Ms. Flowers, Billie, and my dogs. I give the command, "friend," to Yin and Yang, allowing Paul and the kid to enter. My boys are trained to separate me from strangers when I enter the house.

Ms. Flowers who was sitting on the sofa with Nikki and Billie stands abruptly when she sees the kid.

"Dion?" she asks.

I look to the kid, and he looks down. I want to hear him lie now.

"I knew you weren't dead!" She walks to him and embraces him.

He doesn't return the hug, "Dion is dead, Ms. Flowers. My name is Roger Franklyn."

"What? What foolishness are you saying?"

She releases him from the embrace.

"You have mistaken me for someone who is dead."

She steps back, and looks to me questioningly. I have no answer for her.

"What type of charade is this? Who are you trying to fool? You need to tell the police that that was your brother who killed Dr. Aims, and shot Mr. Brown. I have been waiting for you to clear your name. This whole situation is a mess."

"My name is Roger Franklyn!" He snaps, "Dion Jacobs is dead. Don't you understand? Dion is dead!"

He draws back to strike her, but I am closer than he thinks. I catch him by the arm and take him to the floor. Paul gets a little froggy, but my dogs and my brother change his mind. While sitting atop the kid, my first thought is to cause him some pain, pain equal to what Regina felt.

"Kick his ass," comes from Nikki.

The kid is expecting me to hit him. His eyes are squinted tightly closed, and he is moving his head from side to side as if the movement would stop a punch.

I grab his chin to hold his head steady.

"Who the fuck are you? Say your Christen given name, or I will beat you stupid."

I slap him once, so that he can feel my intent.

"Dion Jacobs," he quickly answers, "I was born Dion Jacobs. My brother, Teddy, was killed earlier, but you have to understand, Dion has to be dead for me to work with Victory. And working with Victory is my new beginning. Y'all can't stop that, please, don't. You can't keep me behind. I'll break through being Roger Franklyn."

Since he's talking I got questions, and the main one is, "Who killed the girls?"

"It wasn't us, I swear."

I slap again.

"It wasn't us," he pleads. The kid has no tolerance for pain.

"Dr. Aims was experimenting on the girls!" I yell into his face.

"Yeah, but we didn't kill them. We were helping them. The research worked."

I don't like his answer, so I gesture as if I am going to slap him again.

He spurts out, "The research worked. He cured addiction. At first it worked too damn good."

Confused I ask, "What?"

How could it work too good?

128

"Let me up, Mr. Price, and I will tell you everything."

That's what I want to know, every damn thing, so I raise up and let him up. I pull him over to the couch and sling him to a seat.

Ms. Flowers and Paul join him on the couch. My brother and I take the arm chairs. Nikki and Billie sit on the carpet, each petting a dog.

"Get started," I urge.

"We didn't kill anyone. Dr. Aims' cure worked four years ago with his wife. The problem was it worked too damn good. One dose and the person was no longer an addict. Even if they used again they wouldn't use to the point of compulsion.

"The cure took away the constant desire in one dose. An alcoholic could have one drink. A crack addict could smoke one bag and they would be satisfied. The solution worked like a charm, and that was the problem. Victory didn't want a one dose cure."

"What?" Billie asks from the floor next to me, but all in the room are looking at Dion like he said sand could cure thirst.

"Repeat dosages make the money. They want addicts to take the dosages for at least a year before being cured, the longer the better."

"You have to be kidding!" says Ms. Flowers.

"No. I am not. Making medicine is a business, and that's what was pissing Dr. Aims off. He had the cure, but not the cure they wanted. But they kept giving us money, so we kept working on it, or so I thought.

"We got the house out here on the Southside, and moved girls in for closer observation during the treatment, but they started coming up dead. Just like some of the girls on the Westside, but every girl we worked on the Southside, except you, Billie, came up dead."

"So Claire Anderson was at the house?" I ask.

"Who?"

"Claire Anderson, was she one of the girls at the house?"

"No. We didn't have a Claire."

If Ricky's niece wasn't at the house, that meant she was not getting the cure, but she too got murdered. However, she was a patient of the clinic with the others.

"The deaths, along with the extended research were bumming the doc out. He was talking about taking the cure somewhere else, but I didn't take him serious. Victory had given us so much. My brother found out that the doc was making a deal with another pharmaceutical company, and he was cutting us out all together.

"My brother sold crack on the Westside, and was very valuable to us locating the first test subjects. Because the doc wanted to keep the research secret, we didn't plan on using center patients, but many of the girls my bother brought us were homeless, so we had to house them in the center's shelter. And that's how we got on your books, Ms. Flowers.

"And then the Doc's love for young sisters didn't help things a bit. And then the murders started, and shit just got messy all around on the Westside. After he got fired from the clinic out west, the people at Victory helped us open the house on the Southside. My brother found more girls, and we were back in business. And then, Ms. Flowers, you got him on at another clinic, and things were going good, but I think Doc was just bored with doing the research.

"He had the cure and he wanted the riches. Victory was stalling his lush life. My brother tried to talk to the doc about what he overheard him saying on the phone with another company, and the doc called him Igor. He told him to stay in his place. Doc told him that all he had coming was what he gave him. My brother saw it different, and so did I.

"I called Victory and tricked on the doc. My brother took it to another level. He thought Doc was killing the girls accidently with the cure, and that he was going to blame us for the deaths after he made his new deal. He felt that either Doc was going to pin the murders on him, or leave him broke and back to selling newspapers and ten dollar crack- rocks.

"He was certain that neither the doc nor Victory was going to do a thing for him, so he asked the doc for fifty grand. The doc told him no. He slapped the doc and stole some of the cure and left.

"The next morning, my brother went into the clinic and blew Doc's brains out and that was that. My call was already in to Victory, so they brought me in along with all Doc's files and notes.

"We closed the house down, and the only loose ends were my brother, Billie, and Doc's wife. Victory cut a deal with Doc's wife, and we were looking for Billie when my brother interfered. I don't know what was on his mind. He was trying to stay part of something he really wasn't part of. He knew about the research, but his part was minimal, but he wanted in all the way."

"And Dr. Aims was cutting you in all the way?" I ask.

"Yes, I was there from the first when there was no cure. I brought my brother in because of his access to crack-heads. I guess in reality, he was little more than an Igor."

"And what was you?" Nikki asks him.

"I was his lab assistant. I ran tests, checked specimens, and brought up new ideas. I have a science background."

"So he was including you in the new deal?" I ask.

131

"I never brought it up to him."

"But you brought it up to Victory," Ms. Flowers states.

"It's about survival, not loyalty to the doc. According to my brother the new deal was all Doc's. I wasn't going to bite the hand that fed me. Victory kept us with everything we needed and money. I was drawing an eighty thousand dollar a year salary as Doc's lab assistant. My chances of landing another gig that sweet are slim to none. Yeah, I gave the doc up, and I would do it again.

"Victory Pharmaceutical is taking care of me. They are going to make billions off of Docs' research . . . which I delivered, and all I asked for was a little cash, a new start, and a better education, and they agreed. Roger Franklyn has been accepted to University of California's Pharmacy program with a five year scholarship from Victory. So yes, Dion Jacobs is dead.

"And I hope to God you people don't get the crabs in the barrel syndrome, and pull a brother back down."

"Who do you think killed the girls?" I ask again.

"I don't know, but it wasn't us or Victory Pharmaceuticals."

"If that stuff works so good why did it make me pass out?" Billie asks.

"'Cause you left the house. You only had one dose. Doc figured it out for multiple doses. At least, I think he did. That's up to Victory to find out for sure. My part is done."

"We need to speak to the people at Victory, Ms. Flowers and myself." I tell him.

"Not a problem, they want to talk to y'all too. Well, at least Ms. Flowers."

My house phone rings. I walk over to the lamp table and pick it up.

The caller i.d. displays my neighbor, Fred's, number.

"Hey, D, have you seen the news? They have found another murdered girl."

"Hold on, Fred. Robert, cut on the television."

"Channel nine, D," he directs.

When Robert cuts the television on it's already on channel nine.

The address on the screen is Eighty-fifth and St. Lawrence. I know immediately who the victim is.

Chapter Eighteen

Lee told me to get to her, but the risk was her leaving town not her getting murdered. We all thought the black ribbon killings were over. We were wrong.

Ms. Flowers is riding with me in the rental. Paul and the kid insisted on following us over to the scene.

"You knew her, right?" I ask Ms. Flowers.

Her gaze is out the window on passing traffic, she answers, "Yes, we came to be friends, but obviously not as close as I thought. I had no idea she had taken Dr. Aims' cure. I thought she stopped using through the groups and the meetings. I counted her as a success of our program."

I hear fatigue in her voice. This woman has had a hard couple of days.

"In a sense, she was. Dr. Aims was part of your program."

She exhales heavily and says, "No. Dr. Aims was not part of our treatment plan, and his research certainly wasn't. I want it understood that he and his cure are outside of what we offer at the clinic. Addiction can't be cured in a pill."

"The kid seems to think it can, and so does Victory Pharmaceutical."

"They are wrong, and time will tell as it always does."

I don't say it to her, but I hope she's wrong. I think the world would benefit greatly if addiction could be cured in a pill, even a multiple dose cure.

When we get to Eighty-Fifth Street, I turn into a gas station to get a white T. I forgot to put one on at the house. I don't want to arrive at a crime scene shirtless under my Sox jacket. Ms. Flowers thinks my stopping is funny.

"Buy much of your wardrobe from filling stations do you?"

I start to tell about my account at Fox Brothers, but I let the comment slide with a chuckle. She's seen me dressed. When we get to St. Lawrence the hoopla of the press is over, only the police and a few curious neighbors are seen in the alley. While parking on Eighty-fifth, I spot Lee and Dixon in the alley. I guess they've gotten re-reassigned back to the case. Ms. Flowers has followed me out of the car, and is behind me as I go up the alley to the detectives.

I am expecting Lee to blame me in part for the doctor's wife's death since I didn't get to her in a timely manner. But I feel no guilt in her death because we all thought the murders were over.

I am glad the body is gone because this brother really doesn't want see another corpse.

"Guess it ain't over," Lee says to us looking up from a blue light beam that he is running along the bottom of a fence.

Ms. Flowers stops.

I guess she doesn't want to see anything gross. I proceed to Lee.

Dixon's stern look objects to me being in the alley, but he doesn't say anything. He continues pointing his own blue beam of light onto the edges of the alley.

"Her body was still warm, Price. She had crack-rocks in her pocket along with a crack-pipe, and over ten grand in cash. We found her clothes in a trash can at the other end of the alley. She was found with a black ribbon around her neck, and naked like the others.

"And just to let you know, we found out what actually killed the others as, well . . . they were injected with battery acid. The same composition in all the victims, the murderer has been dipping out the same battery since the Westside killings. Sick fuck."

He looks from the bottom of the fence to me, "So how is your buddy Ricky Brown doing?"

"He's doing fine, out of intensive care and in a regular room."

"Good. So what you got on this, Price, anything we don't know?"

Now that is a strange question from a cop. I have never had him or any other cop ask me what I had in regards to an ongoing investigation. They usually want me to think they know everything, and they pretend they know what I'm trying to keep secret. An honest question from a cop, I answer with, "It ain't the doc's research."

Since we both knew of the doc's research and didn't speak on it, I start with it.

"You talked to the people at Victory?" He steps closer to me and his blue light lands at my feet.

"Not exactly, but a very convincing source all the same."

I don't say Dion/Roger's name because I don't want to be the crab in the barrel that pulls him down. If the kid can get a fresh start in this world, who am I to deny it.

"Oh, so where you at?" He asks again.

He asks this as if we are teammates, or brothers-in-arms with the same objective. Me on the same team as a cop, Ricky would get a kick out of this, but the truth of the situation is we do have the same objective. We want the murders to stop.

"I think it's community based, a sicko in the 'hood."

"I agree," he says clicking off the flash light.

"I'm pointing my efforts around the clinics, both the Westside one and the Southside one."

"I think those effort will be well served." He said patting me on my shoulder.

This is the first time he has ever touched me. I take a step back out of his arm reach. I don't want him touching me again. The motherfucker is still sleeping with Regina, and he ain't my buddy. Sharing an objective doesn't make us friends.

"What about you and your partner?" I ask.

"I was thinking Dion Jacobs, but that went nowhere. My partner was thinking . . ." he quickly looks in Ms. Flower's direction, "or another employee. We are targeting the clinics too."

I don't have enough confidence in Ms. Flowers to argue in her defense, so I say, "Good hunting," and turn to leave.

When I get to the mouth of the alley, Ms. Flowers says, "Mr. Price, Linda Williams' grandfather stays down the street. If you don't mind I would like to stop by and express my condolences."

"It's kind of late?"

"Mr. Williams won't mind."

*

And he didn't. The tall older gentleman with a shaved head went as far as to fix us cups of coffee which I took despite the late hour.

"I lived here when this neighborhood was mostly Italian. We raised Linda's mama and nine other kids under this roof. My wife died here, and I'm planning to do the same. A couple of my kids are trying to get me to sell the house, and move to a senior citizen's home, I keep telling them I got a home. They telling me the house is worth three hundred thousand dollars. I paid twelve for it.

"I figure if it's worth all that it should be worth more after I die this year or next, and that's more money for them. From the ten of them I got sixteen grandchildren. Three hundred thousand dollars ought to leave everybody a nice piece of change."

Mr. Williams has sat in his kitchen at his yellow Formica topped round table. He smiles, sipping from his 'Number 1 Gramps' mug. His two top teeth have been outlined in gold, and the metal catches light from the overhead florescent above the kitchen table.

"Linda was my ninth grandchild. She left here this afternoon going out to take care of some business. The girl came here with a suitcase full of money; it's up front on the couch. I didn't tell the police nothing about it, figured the family could use it just as much as the city.

"The detective told me they found ten thousand dollars in her pocket. They will be serving ice water in hell before we see a dime of that money. I worked for the city for fifty-three years. I know how things go downtown. How is the coffee?" He smiles to Ms. Flowers.

"It's good, sir. Do you know where Linda was going to conduct her business?" Ms. Flowers asks, and I am surprised because it is the same question I was gonna ask.

"She was settling accounts, that much I know. She'd been up to that all day. She had a ticket to Aruba, that doctor husband of hers bought them a nice house down there. That's where she was heading to, but she had a couple favors to make good on. She wanted to help those that had helped her. You know Linda was on that stuff pretty bad for a long while, Ms. Flowers, until she met y'all and the doc. Y'all turned her around sure enough."

He nods his head agreeing with his own statement. "She got to live free of that stuff for awhile at least. I figure her going back around her old associates got her caught in some kind of mess. You got to let some sleeping dogs lie. I told her to mail them people post cards from Aruba, and forget about them, but she wouldn't hear it, wanted to spread her blessings on those that had helped her."

He pushes his chair back from the table. I see tears welling in his eyes, "I got some left over catfish if you two are hungry. Her mama should be here shortly. Their flight landed at ten-fifteen over at Midway. She's going to rent a car, and drive over here. She never liked riding in taxis. I think she's too bossy to let anybody else drive her. Linda's mama is my oldest girl, and she is as bossy as my wife was.

"Well, I'm going to lay down some, you two are welcome to stay and wait for her, but I got put these old bones down."

He slowly rises from the table as he extends his home to us.

"Thanks for your time, sir, but we're going to be leaving. There is no need for us to speak to Linda's mother, and you have our deepest condolences."

Again, I couldn't have said it better.

The picture Mr. Williams has painted of Linda is different from the one I had in my mind from talking to Onita and Ms. Flowers. I had her pegged as an opportunist, a gold digger, not someone who would make good on debts, or share her windfall. And the police finding a crack-pipe and crack-rocks in her clothes didn't help my mental image of her at all. But her grandfather makes me feel her passing and his loss.

"All right then, y'all write your phone number on the note pad by the phone, and I'll call you with the funeral arrangements."

At the door I tell him, "Mr. Williams I am going to do my best to find out who is killing our daughters."

Looking down at me he shakes my hand and says, "You just be careful, young man, and remember God is in control. He runs things down here. It may not be in His plan for you find out who is doing all this wrong no matter how bad you want to find out. Some things is better off left alone. I tried to tell Linda the same thing. What we want, ain't always what's best for us. Now you both take care."

*

In the car I tell Ms. Flowers, "We need to find out where she went. There is a link between the Westside and the Southside killings and it's getting missed by me and the police. Linda was from the Westside, but she got killed out here. Whoever she went to visit is the link if not the murderer."

"What do you mean link?"

"The link has to be someone who was connected to the girls on both sides of the city, somebody other than the doc and his crew."

"That just leaves the clinics, Mr. Price, nothing else connects them."

"Why did the girls come to the clinics?"

"For treatment?"

"What kind of treatment?"

"Drug treatment."

"Drugs, that is the common thread."

I start the car.

"We need to get into the traveling circle of drug users. We need to talk to Nikki, Billie, and my brother. They probably know some dealer or some addict who lived on both sides of the city, somebody who Linda could have had dealings with. Somebody she owed a debt to."

"That's dangerous mental terrain for them."

"It was dangerous for Linda, too. It was dangerous for Babygirl, and all the other young sisters we have lost to this piece of-shit murderer. They just gonna have to man-up."

Chapter Nineteen

We walk into the house and are greeted by Yin and Yang only. My brother, Nikki, and Billie are absent. I search through the house leaving Ms. Flowers in the living area. I come up empty, not even a note.

My mind doesn't go to the possibility that they are in danger. My thinking goes to the money Billie said she had, and my brother's and Nikki's recent drug using relapse. Billie wanted to get high, and I left her with two backsliders. Damn, what was I thinking?

"They are gone, aren't they?" Ms. Flowers asks when I return to the living area.

"Yep. Up like Chuck."

"Any idea where?"

"The dope house down the block is my guess."

"Should we go there?"

"I'm not. They grown and they doing what they want to do. I am tired of crack-heads."

And I am. When is enough enough? A maniac is out there killing female crack-heads, and these fools go out and get high, and one of them is a known target. If they're not concerned, why should I be?

As soon as I have the thought, I see Babygirl, and her mother's anguished face. My mind answers the question of why be concerned. What's happening is bigger than the missing three. My concern is for the safety of the community, my area, and my space. This killer is in my circle, and I want the crazy fucker gone.

"It's a disease, Mr. Price. They are not out there by choice. Yes, it may appear as if they made a choice, but they really didn't."

"It's three of them." I say, "One of them could have tried to stop

143

the others. One of them could have stayed behind."

"Which one, which addict would you have not be an addict for your convenience? Your brother? He should have been the one? You think he should have been stronger than the two weak females and save the day?"

Her eyebrows rise, and her face questions me.

I hadn't thought about that directly, but once she says it, I agree with her. I do think my brother should have redirected the thought, and yes, I feel the safety of the two women should have outweighed his want to get high.

So I tell her, "Yeah, I think that!"

The questioning expression changes to a smirk, into the slight smile that one gives a child that doesn't know that the pretty bumble bee is not to be played with.

"The disease of addiction doesn't recognize gender, Mr. Price. If your brother had cancer would you expect him to battle it stronger than a woman? Would you think his muscles would give him a better chance at survival? They would not, and they do not in addiction either.

"No, addiction wouldn't allow him to be the hero. Once the opportunity to get high became available, little rational thought prevailed, only addicted thinking.

"Thinking motivated by the thought of obtaining drugs. It may be better that they are together, perhaps together some rational thought may surface that may be convenient for you."

She said it again. For my convenience, no, it was for the convenience of ending the case. I really don't care what type of thinking is in play. I need them here to move forward. To get the names of some people Linda may have known on this side of town, to go to some of the places, to move forward. But no, they have stagnated my movement by getting high.

"Whatever," is my reply. "You need to move your car though. Seeing you parked in front of the house will stop them from coming in. They can easily lie to me. You are a harder challenge."

"Yes, I agree, where should I park?"

"I'm going to open the garage for you."

*

She drives down the decline into the garage with no problem. The navy blue Volvo looks good under the bright lights of the garage and so does she. Her honey brown skin, a shade lighter than my own, is smooth and evenly toned. She really is a good looking woman. I am surprised she isn't married.

Damn, looking at her car puts my BMW on my mind. I need to report the accident to my insurance company. My Beamer is history.

"Are you okay, Mr. Price? Suddenly you look horribly sad. I am sure they will return soon."

I don't have the heart to tell her it's my wrecked car and not the missing three that is responsible for my expression. I extend my hand to help her up the two stairs into my house.

*

Ms. Flowers won't relax, and her edginess has my dogs on alert. Me, I am chill because a brother made a call. She and I are looking at CNN, but my thoughts are not on world news, my thinking is local.

For the past ten minutes she has been trying to convince me to go down the block and get the three.

"We have been back for thirty minutes and chances are they went down there as soon as we left. Waiting for them to come back on their

145

own is a mistake. We should go get them, Mr. Price."

I haven't told her about the call because it's not the type of call I want anyone to know I made. The doorbell rings, and she and my dogs spring to attention. I go to door, and see Paul and Dion/Roger.

Paul says, "We figured the invitation was still good and we bought chicken." He holds up a Harold's Chicken Shack bag.

Worrying about the three has caused his surveillance of Ms. Flowers to slip my mind all together. I open the door allowing them to enter. Looking out into the street I see my brother with Nikki and Billie hurriedly making it toward my house. I look down the block and see people exiting the Reeds like a bomb threat was announced. My call worked.

Detective Lee pulls up in front of my house while the three are climbing the stairs. He rolls down the window, nods, and pulls off. If you have a cop on your team you might as well use him. What is the use of having a big man on the squad and not putting him in the hole?

*

The three aren't hungry but Paul, Ms. Flowers, Dion/Roger, and me are digging into the chicken while sitting at my grandmama's kitchen table.

Again, Claire enters my mind. I should have kept backtracking her steps. I let the shooting throw me off. Ricky and I had agreed that the streets held the answers. Crack-heads knew the link.

Looking at Ms. Flowers I ask, "Do you know where Claire was staying when she first came to the clinic?"

"I'm not certain, because after a day or so I was able to get her back with her family. Why?"

"She was staying with an old guy named Jumpy," I tell her.

"Jumpy? I have heard the name. A few of our girls have mentioned it, including Billie."

"What about on the Westside, did any girls out West mention his name?"

"I'm not certain, why?"

"Because he lived on the Westside, and he's living out here now. We went to see him yesterday when we were backtracking Claire. Ricky remembered him from the Westside. It seems he trades a place to stay for sex."

I finish off the chicken breast, and walk up front to Billie.

She is sitting alone on the couch watching BET videos. I hear my brother and Nikki talking in his room. To Billie I say, "I need you to tell me about Ole Jumpy. I saw you leaving his place yesterday." I sit next to her on the couch.

"Ain't much to tell, he's an old freak that hates for girls to leave him. Always talking about how much he does for women, but he always got his dick in his hand."

"What happened with him and Claire?"

"Oh, he was crazy about her. Let her sleep in his room all while she was there. He thought she was going to stay for awhile. He tripped when she left, didn't want to be bothered with nobody. He wouldn't even get high. He got like that when one of his favorites left. He would go off for a day or so then come back and be his regular horny-dog self."

"Were you one of his favorites?" I ask.

"No, I was too old, had too much mouth for him, and too much pussy. I like to fuck after getting my pussy ate. All Jumpy wanted to do, or could do, was eat the pussy. If he did get hard he came right

147

away, and I talked about his three-minute ass in front of the girls. No, I wasn't one of his favorites. But he let me stay as long as I acted like I needed his ass. He loves to be needed."

"The other two girls that died before Claire, did you know them? Did they live there with him?"

She sits up straight, "Yeah they did. Damn, I never thought about it because so many people be in and out of his place. And you know what else, Mr. Price? They was all his favorites, and they all left him after they started taking the doc's cure.

"Damn, it's fuckin' Jumpy!" She stands up from the couch and yells, "Nikki! It's fuckin' Jumpy!"

Yes, she is jumping to a conclusion, but I am too. I can see the little game-less pervert doing it. He had been losing the girls to the cure. They weren't addicted, so they didn't need him. When he found out Claire was going to the clinic he figured the doc would give her the cure too. He told us the doc had her to throw us off his trail. That sick fuck. I should have let Ricky put a bullet in his twisted brain. Damn!

*

I had Ms. Flowers call the doctor's wife's grandfather, and Mr. Williams more than confirmed that his granddaughter knew Neal Henson. He told Ms. Flowers that she lived with him on the Westside, and he thought that if Linda was making good on debts, Neal Henson would be a stop for sure.

I strapped on my pistols and left everybody at the house, ignoring all protest. I am not sure how things are going to turn out, but I need to see this man alone without the police. I'm not a killer. His death isn't on my mind, but I need to see him without the police.

Hell, he might be innocent for all I know. No sense in sending

Detective Lee on a wild goose chase. I just want to talk to Ole Jumpy, and see if he will confess to me. See if he can convince me that he didn't do it. That is all I want to do.

When I get about two blocks from Jumpy's block, I see nothing but squad cars and press. I can't even get near his block. I look in the rearview mirror to back up and see Paul's SUV behind me. They followed me despite me telling them to stay put. The press and more police are behind his SUV. We are gridlocked. It's a damn circus.

I pull out my phone and call Lee.

"You got him?"

"Yep, we got him with a full confession, and a big spool of black funeral ribbon, and a photo album of the victims. The sick fuck took pictures of the corpses. Dixon found a car battery in his bedroom closet, and get this . . . the sick fuck is a diabetic. We found plenty of needles in his bedroom. We got him, thanks to you, Price."

"Thanks to me? How so?"

"Look on your left jacket sleeve."

I do, and see what looks like a burnt match head stuck on my Sox jacket. I pull it off.

"You bugged me!"

"Yep, I tagged you in the alley. You ain't a cop, Price. Stop acting like one!" And the bastard clicks off.

Ain't that a bitch, we solve the case and his ass gets the credit by eavesdropping. I flick the match-head-looking device out the window. I think about what Mr. Williams said, 'God is in control down here.' Who knows what would have happened had I got to Ole Jumpy first. Lee is right, I am not a cop.

I pull out my phone and dial Ricky's sister, Brenda's number.

"We got him, Brenda, and this time it is the real killer."

"Is he alive?"

"Yes, the police caught him, not me."

"Thank you, Jesus! And you sure he is the one?"

"No doubt in my mind."

"Good. I'll tell Reynard."

"Good night now." And I hang up.

Ricky's promise made good.

The traffic still has me gridlocked on the block, so I dial Carol's number to catch her up, and to tell her that I will be in to work in the p.m. A brother needs to get some real sleep.

"Hey," she answers on the second ring.

"Hey, yourself, we caught the bastard."

"Very good, who was it?"

"A old guy with issues."

"An old guy . . . really? I thought they were sex crimes too?"

"Not really sex crimes, but old guys can commit sex crimes."

"I guess. Are they certain of the accused this time?"

"No doubt this time, I'm coming in to work tomorrow in the afternoon."

"You sure you have no more city-saving to do?"

"Nope, the city is safe for tonight."

"Did you call Regina?"

I hadn't. Oh my God, not once.

"No. I should do that now."

"Yeah, you should. See you tomorrow, D."

I was dialing the hospital when Ms. Flowers opens the door of the rental car and gets in.

"My surveilers have been called off the case. It seems with the murderer caught, I am no longer of interest to Victory Pharmaceuticals. Am I still of interest to you, Mr. Price? I hope I am, at least interesting enough to get a ride back to my car." She gets in and closes the 300's door.

Is she of interest to me? She was yesterday, even entered a dream. I look at her honey brown complexion, and straight black hair, and think about what Billie said about being one of Ole Jumpy's favorites. She had too much mouth to be one of his favorites. It wasn't that Ms. Flowers had too much mouth. I like women to challenge me, but Ms. Flowers turned me off because of her relationship with Dr. Aims. Either she was in denial about Dr. Aims' research, and his trading sex for prescriptions. Or worse, she ignored the facts. I believe the latter.

She knew all about Dr. Aims' research and his sexual acts, but went along with both to keep him as a physician working at the clinic, letting him experiment on and take advantage of her own kind. And that shit just ain't right.

I don't dial Regina's hospital number. Looking into the rearview mirror, I see that the police are clearing traffic. I tell the pretty Ms. Flowers, "Yep, I think you are interesting enough to get a ride to your car."

Chapter Twenty

In the morning the headline reads, 'Actual Black Ribbon Murderer Caught.' The story is reported by Regina Price. I guess she was doing good enough to make her deadline. When I called the hospital last night, she had been released. I am referred to in the article as an executive from Epsilon Security Service, and Ricky is referred to as a consultant to Epsilon Security. Carol will probably get a kick out the company name being mentioned.

I thought I would have been able to sleep through the morning, but I can't. A brother really didn't sleep good at all. I feel like I am leaving something undone, like something isn't finished with the case. I reason that it is because I haven't actually talked to Ricky and wrapped things up with him.

It's Thursday morning, but it feels like a Sunday morning. The house it quiet, and I really don't want to get out of the bed. I crept past Billie sleeping on the couch, and got the paper off the porch, and brought it back to the bed with me. Ms. Flowers left last night without coming back into the house.

When I came in, nobody said anything about leaving, we all talked about how obvious it was that Ole Jumpy was the killer once the facts were laid out. Hindsight is twenty-twenty, I told them, but only Billie seemed to understand what I meant by it.

Looking at the clock on the night table, I see it's ten-thirty, way too late to be lying around. Regina hasn't returned my call. I bet she returned Lee's. He probably picked her up from the hospital, bastard. I'm flipping the paper to the sport pages when I hear a soft tap on the door.

"Yeah?"

The door opens, and Billie walks in naked as a Jaybird.

"Them two are downstairs going at it like bunnies, getting a bitch all hot and bothered. I started to go in and join them until I remembered you was up here. Why share when I can have a whole man to myself."

She closes my bedroom door behind her, and hops right into my bed. Under my robe, I too am naked as a Jaybird, and the sight of her taut little body does stir me.

I sit up and say, "Wait a minute," but I don't push her out of the bed, and neither do I get out.

"Why? I'm clean. Every girl at the center gets checked out." She nestles up next to me. "Oh, you a muscle man for real."

Her thin wavy hair is under my chin and it is silky soft. She kisses my chest, and her hands run across my abs.

She pulls my robe, and despite me thinking this ain't right, my jones is growing to the attention position.

"How old are you?" I ask, not sure of how I am going to respond if she says something like twenty-two. My blood is going too, and my thinking is coming from my smaller head. She smells like soap and strawberries, and her hair so damn soft.

"I'm twenty-eight, twenty-nine in two days. I know you ain't worried about me being legal. That's sweet if you are. Oh, look at you." She says about the state of my jones, "I hope you ain't a three-minute-brother, 'cause I needs all of that up in me, and I want it there for a while. A good-ass while."

Half a man's age plus seven. I heard that somewhere. That is a good way to determine if a woman is too young to mess with. I am forty-one. She's twenty-eight. Half is twenty plus seven. She's old enough. But damn, she has issues. I should push her away, but she has my jones in her hands. And we are enjoying her touch.

"You gonna like this head, wait and see."

Fuck it. I need it, and she wants it, so there it is.

*

I more than liked the head, and I stayed in her longer than awhile. I stayed in her so long that we both fell asleep and didn't wake up until three-fifteen, and we wouldn't have woke up then, but my brother has brought a pizza to the room.

"Thought y'all might be a little hungry," he says grinning at me while standing at the foot of the bed with pizza in hand, "me and Nikki ordered y'all one too."

I don't ask him where he got the money because I really don't care. I am starving, and glad he thought about us. He puts the pizza on the bed, and leaves while pulling the door up behind him, "I let the dogs out, and Nikki fed them."

Billie pulled the covers up around us when he knocked on the door, and I liked that. Once the door is closed she strips them back, and I find my eyes on her small breasts, flat stomach, and muscular thighs. She is built like a runner. She hustles down to the pizza and gets herself a slice and brings me back one too. She lays with the back of her head on my chest while she eats her slice. I chew above her.

Looking at her youthful face, it's hard to believe she is twenty-eight, but after sharing my bed with her, I know for certain that she is a grown-ass woman. A grown-ass woman who has slept with my brother, and who would have gone into the room with him and his girl if I hadn't been available. I sho' am glad I was available, damn glad.

"Let's not talk," she says between chews, "let's just eat this and then do it some more. Okay?"

I answer her by licking the tomato sauce off her lips.

*

"Man, you got to be kiddin' me. You left her in yo' crib? Wid yo' flat screen, watches, and jewelry? Nigga, is you crazy?"

Ricky is flat on his back, doctor's orders, talking up to me from his hospital bed. I have to stand to see his face while he's talking.

"When you goin' stop lettin' a little trim turn you stupid? Why didn't she go to da group with yo' brother and da other little crack-head?"

"She doesn't go to the center anymore for treatment."

"Oh, she ain't even tryin' to get help . . . and you goin' fo' dat? Man, she must of whipped it on you good. She ain't big as a minute, and has no ass at all. What . . . you like her wavy hair or somethin'? Man, you too old to be pussy-whipped. You need to get back to da crib and check on yo' stuff."

"Everything ain't based on material things, Ricky. Sometimes extending trust helps a person."

And I believe that. There is nothing in my house that cannot be replaced, but the simple act of trusting my house to her might build up something in her more valuable than a T.V. or watch.

"You trust people after dey have shown you somethin'. All dis girl did was give you some pussy, and you left her yo' whole crib."

Changing the subject because what he is saying is disturbing me a bit, I ask, "Have they got a date for Babygirl's services?"

"Yeah, Brenda pushin' things back till Monday evenin'. Da doctors say I should be out by Saturday afternoon. She's real proud of you, D. Bragged on you to all of da nurses when she came here dis afternoon. I told her we had da creep earlier, but you wouldn't let me shoot him.

156

"She said Reynard ain't left da house yet. He won't go up to da funeral parlor to see da body or nothin'. He told Brenda he wasn't goin' to da funeral."

"He'll come around," I say.

"I don't know. Dat man don't waiver. What he says he does."

I lower my hand to my best friend's shoulder, "How long are you going to be on your back?"

"Dey suppose to sit me up dis evenin', after da gut doctor gives da okay. Dey said da bleedin' has stopped on da insides. How you doin'?" He twists a little under the sheet obviously uncomfortable.

"I'm good, no stitches just cuts and bruises."

"How Regina?"

"Good too. She wrote the story for the paper."

"How y'all date go?"

"Didn't happen, ain't gonna happen."

"Told cha."

"Whatever, man."

"Yo partner stopped by here to see me. Ms. Carol brought me flowers, and a book on positive thinkin'. The book tickled Martha. Oh, check dis out. I lost seven pounds."

"Ricky, you got shot."

"I know that. I'm just sayin', seven pounds is seven pounds. Dat put me under four hundred. It's goin' to have to be all about diet until I heal better on da inside. Can't do much exercisin'. I'ma go wid da no-carb one first. Dis here weight comin' off me. You can bet dat."

"I hear you, brother."

"You gonna ride wid me and Martha to da service?"

"Yeah, I'm pretty sure I will."

157

"You bringin' yo new roommate?"

"See you tomorrow, Ricky."

"Peace, my brother."

*

I had called Carol from home and told her I wouldn't make it to the office until after closing. She told me to get some rest, and that she would see me in the morning. When I pull up to our building, I am surprised to see her little Benz still here. I am more surprised to see her and Keith sitting in the front seat kissing, and I mean they are going at it, heads twisting and their arms around each other, the whole nine yards.

I start to hit my bright lights and honk my horn, but I don't. I back up, and drive right past them unnoticed. Whatever I was going to catch up on this evening can be caught up on in the morning. Carol got herself a boyfriend, and I didn't even see it coming.

My cell phone rings, and I see Ms. Flowers' number.

"Mr. Price, I wanted you to be one of the first know. Victory Pharmaceutical has renewed the grant for the children's shelter, and has offered us two more substantial grants for the running of the clinic. Isn't that wonderful?" she chirps.

At what cost is my thought.

"Are they going to continue the research in the city?"

"No, from my understanding they are moving it to a university in California. But Dr. Jerome Benson said the clinic will be funded through Victory well into the future."

"He called you?"

"No, not initially. He returned my call after I left a message about having a list of Dr. Aims' research patients from both the Westside and

Southside clinics. That's the information I went out West to gather last night. It didn't seem ethical to me that research should be conducted in such a fashion, nor should it have been funded in secret. I left a message saying as much and within an hour I got the call from Victory." She laughs.

"And in addition, the University of Illinois, Chicago, has agreed to temporarily staff us with a physician and interns until we can find a permanent replacement for Dr. Aims. Oh, what a difference a day makes. Last night things appeared so grim, but this evening the sky is the limit. I just wanted to share the progress with you."

"Well, I am glad you did, and I am happy for you and the clinic."

"Thank you, and have a good evening. And please remind Robert and Nikki that they are expected at the evening meeting."

"Will do."

She made the best of a bad situation, and the community still has a clinic. But the cost was high, too damn high. When I pull up to my house, I park blocking my driveway because I see a Lincoln navigator parking in front of my house.

Regina, Lee, and my son, Chester, climb out of the SUV. My son has on overalls, and a long-sleeved yellow sweatshirt. I love the sight of the boy even if his mother does get him wack soup-bowl haircuts.

"Hey, Daddy Man!" he screams and runs to me.

I pick my son up and hug him tight.

"Ouch! You gonna squish my insides out. Why you hug so hard all the time?"

"Because I don't see you enough, and I be trying to smash you into me so we'll be together always."

"That won't work, Daddy Man. People can't smash into each other.

159

Can they, mommy?"

Lee and Regina are standing next to us. She has one of Chester's backpacks in her hand. Lee's dreadlocks are down around his shoulders, and the punk is in jeans and a White Sox jacket. Who wears a White Sox jacket? Only losers.

"Maybe you can ask your daddy to explain it later."

I look at her, then at the backpack in her hand. She has her hair pulled back in a pony tail and is wearing a pink Bulls jacket. Who wears a pink Bulls jacket? Two losers. They deserve each other.

"I got a couple days off from the paper and Johnny does too. We were thinking about Vegas for a couple of days?" Both of them are in jeans and gym shoes. Dressed for travel is my guess.

I take the backpack from her hands and say, "See you when you get back," and climb the stairs with my son in my arms.

"Bye Mommy and Uncle Johnny."

As we walk through the front door, he waves goodbye and I tell him, "He ain't your uncle. You have an Uncle Robert, an Uncle Charles, and an Uncle Ricky. Johnny is your mama's friend. You call him Mr. Johnny, or Mr. Lee. Got it?"

"Okay, Daddy Man."

I put him down in the living area and he runs straight to the dogs screaming, "My puppies," and the three tumble on the floor.

Billie is sitting on the couch doing her toenails, and watching high school girl's tennis.

"Hey, little man, what's your name?" she asks my son.

"Chester Price," my son answers while being licked to laughter by Yin and Yang.

"Boy, you sure look like David."

"That's because he is my daddy. But my grandmother says it's okay that I look like him, because I'm going to be smarter than him, so looking like him is okay."

I hear my brother and Nikki in the kitchen. I ask Billie, "What's going on in there?"

"They suppose to be making a pot roast for dinner?"

"You ain't helping?"

"I don't cook. I was going to clean your house, but the service came. Then I was going to walk your dogs, but they too big. I couldn't think of anything to do, so I went shopping brought some clothes and a couple of other girly items. I was gonna buy you something, but I bought us something instead."

"What?"

"It's upstairs on the bed. I'ma wear it tonight."

She smiles and I smile back at her.

The truth of this situation is that this woman makes me feel good, and until that changes . . . it is what it is. If she said she went shopping, she went shopping. She does have on new jeans and a red sweater, so she probably did go shopping. If she didn't, fuck it. Our thing is based on feeling good. If things change then things will change.

And the same is true with my brother, when I feel uncomfortable with his actions . . . he is out of here. He is a grown-ass man, and I am not about to be caught up in monitoring his comings and goings. He should know what's best for him. I know what's best for me, and if I feel what is best for me is being threatened . . . changes have to be made.

"What's your name?" Chester asks her while petting Yang.

"My name is Billie."

161

"Billie?" He looks at her intently and says, "That's a boy's name."

"Not if it's on a girl."

And that cracks my son up. He stretches out on the floor in laughter.

"She got a boy's name, Daddy Man."

"Yeah, but she's a woman, a very pretty woman."

And that cracks my son up more.

"Daddy Man said you pretty, Billie. So you a pretty girl with a boy's name." He sits up from the floor and looks to her again, "But that's okay, 'cause I like your name, Billie, it's easy to say."

He stares at her painted toenails and asks, "Where are your shoes?"

"Upstairs in my room."

"You got a room in Daddy Man's house?"

I look to her as well because I want to hear this answer. I'm cool with her being here, but nothing has been discussed.

"Yes, I sleep in Daddy Man's room with him," she answers my son, but her eyes are questioning me.

"Ooh, I feel sorry for you, because Daddy Man farts loud and long when he first wakes up."

Billie laughs.

"I know, and it's stinky. Real stinky," she says pinching her nose closed.

And that sends my son rolling on the floor in a fit of pure laughter. Both dogs pounce on him, and Billie stands from the couch and comes to me.

"I don't like being a secret. I want the world to know that I am sharing your bed. Do you mind?"

Her eyes are still questioning me.

162

"Nope . . . not at all."

"You do plan on me being around longer than a day or two, don't you?"

She rests her hand on my chest.

"Yeah, I am looking forward to us getting to know one another. See how compatible we are outside of the bed."

"Yeah, 'cause we sho' makes it happen in the bed. I ain't been satisfied like that in a long time, Daddy Man."

Smiling, she rises up on her red-polished tippy toes, and kisses me on the lips.

CPSIA information can be obtained at www.ICGtesting.com
Printed in the USA
LVOW08s1516230616

493837LV00002B/217/P